FUN學美國各學科 Preschool 閱讀課本 二版

AMERICAN SCHOOL TEXTBOOK

Reading Key 4

Preschool
介系詞篇

作者 ◎ Michael A. Putlack & e-Creative Contents
譯者 ◎ 歐寶妮

Authors

Michael A. Putlack

Michael A. Putlack graduated from Tufts University in Medford, Massachusetts, USA, where he got his B.A. in History and English and his M.A. in History. He has written a number of books for children, teenagers, and adults.

e-Creative Contents

A creative group that develops English contents and products for ESL and EFL students.

FUN學美國各學科 Preschool 閱讀課本 二版

AMERiCAN SCHOOL TEXTBOOK

Reading Key

4

Preschool
介系詞篇

WORKBOOK
練習本

Workbook

A Cat In the Box

A Read and write.

1. 

box

box

2. 

basket

basket

3. 

table

table

4. 

chair

chair

B Match and write.

1. in the basket

in the basket

2. on the table

on the table

3. under the table

under the table

4. by the chair

by the chair

C Circle the correct word for each sentence.

1.

There is a cat (**in, on**) the box.

2.

There is a cat (**in, on**) the box.

3.

The dog is (**by, under**) the chair.

4.

The dog is (**by, under**) the chair.

D Choose and write.

by　　on　　in　　under

1.

Where is the cat?

It is __by__ the dog.

2.

Where is the dog?

It is _____ the basket.

3.

Where is the dog?

It is ______ the table.

4.

Where is the cat?

It is _________ the chair.

A Cat Next To the Box

A Read and write.

1. 

in front of

in front of

2. 
behind

behind

3. 
next to

next to

4. 
between

between

B Match and write.

1. bedroom — bedroom
2. living room — living room

3. sofa — sofa
4. bed — bed

5. lamp — lamp
6. TV — TV

C Circle the correct word or words for each sentence.

1. The sofa is (**in front of, behind**) the table.
2. The table is (**in front of, behind**) the sofa.

3. The sofa is (**next to, between**) the two lamps.
4. The lamps are (**next to, between**) the sofa.

D Choose and write.

between behind in front of next to

1.

Where are the chairs?

They are __behind__ the table.

2.

Where is the table?

It is ________ the bed.

3.

Where is the chair?

It is ________ the desk.

4.

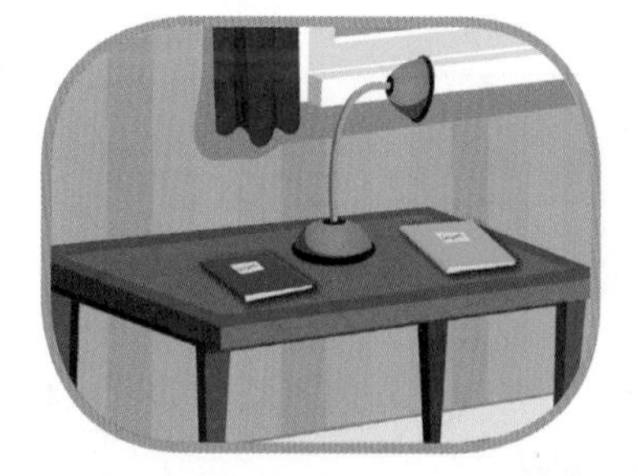

Where is the lamp?

It is ________ the two books.

DAILY TEST

A Cat Below the Tree

A Read and write.

1.

below

below

2.

above

above

3.

beside

beside

4.

on the right

on the right

5.

on the left

on the left

B Match and write.

1. school — school
2. church — church
3. post office — post office
4. supermarket — supermarket

C Circle the correct word or words for each sentence.

1. The bird is (**below, above**) the church.
2. The church is (**below, above**) the bird.

3. The school is (**on the right, on the left**) of Ann.
4. The church is (**below, beside**) the school.

D Choose and write.

beside   above   on the left   on the right

1. Where is the church?
   It is ___**beside**___ the house.
2. Where is the supermarket?
   It is ______________ of the house.
3. Where is the post office?
   It is ______________ of the church.
4. Where is the balloon?
   It is __________ the house.

Inside and Outside

A Read and write.

1. inside

inside

2. outside

outside

3. near

near

4. far from

far from

B Match and write.

1. bus stop — bus stop
2. car — car
3. bus — bus
4. bank — bank
5. post office — post office
6. school — school

C Circle the correct word or words for each sentence.

1. Tom is (**inside, outside**) the bus.
2. Ann is (**inside, outside**) the bus.

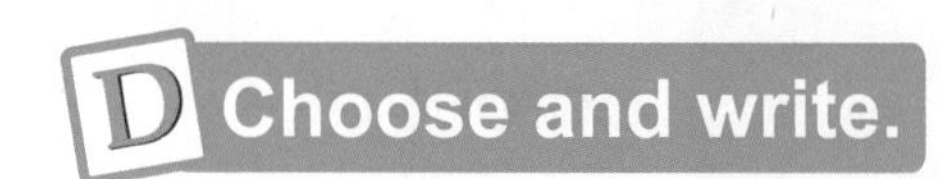

3. John is (**near, far from**) the bus stop.
4. Jane is (**near, far from**) the bus stop.

D Choose and write.

inside outside near far from

1.

Is he **inside** the car?
Yes, he is.

2.

Is she ________ the car?
Yes, she is.

3.

Where is the post office?
It is ________ the bank.

4.

Where is Tom?
He is ________ the post office.

Up and Down

A Read and write.

1. 

go up

go up

2. 

go down

go down

3. 

go into

go into

4. 

go out of

go out of

B Match and write.

1. stairs — stairs
2. elevator — elevator
3. pool — pool 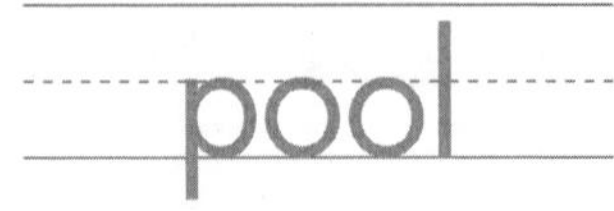
4. hill — hill

C Circle the correct word or words for each sentence.

1.

Ben is going (**up, down**) the hill.

2.

Tom is going (**up, down**) the hill.

3.

Jane is going (**into, out of**) the pool.

4.

Sam is going (**into, out of**) the pool.

D Choose and write.

going down   going up   going into   going out of

1.

What is he doing?
He is **going up** the stairs.

2.

What is she doing?
She is ______________ the stairs.

3.

What is she doing?
She is ______________ the water.

4.

What is it doing?
It is ______________ the water.

Across and Over

A Read and write.

1.

go across

go across

2.

go around

go around

3.

go over

go over

4.

go through

go through

B Match and write.

1. street street
2. corner corner
3. track track
4. tunnel tunnel
5. gate gate

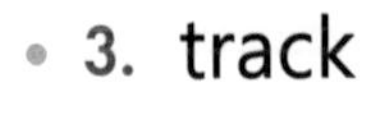

C Circle the correct word for each sentence.

1. 

Jane is going (**across**, **around**) the street.

2. 

Tom is going (**across, around**) the corner.

3. 

He is going (**over, through**) the bar.

4. The bus is going (**over, through**) the gate.

D Choose and write.

going around   going across   going over   going through

1. 

What is he doing?

⇨ He is **going around** the track.

2. What is she doing?

⇨ She is ________________ the finish line.

3. 

What are they doing?

⇨ They are ________________ the street.

4. 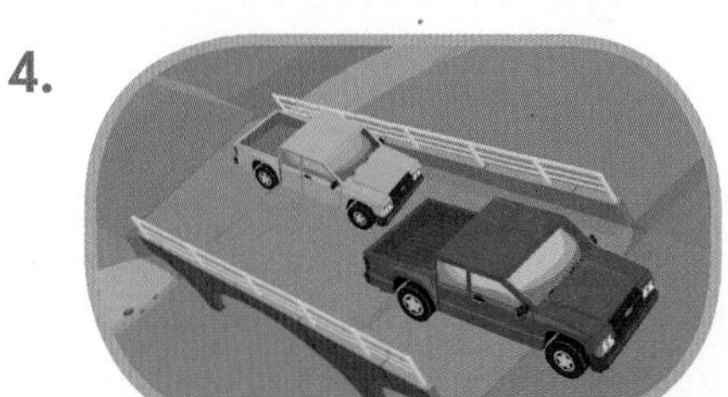

What are the cars doing?

⇨ They are ________________ the bridge.

In, On, At

A Read and write.

1. 

in the morning

in the morning

2. 

in the afternoon

in the afternoon

3. 

in the evening

in the evening

4. 

at night

at night

B Match and write.

1. get up — get up
2. have breakfast — have breakfast
3. go to school — go to school
4. go to church — go to church
5. go to bed — go to bed
6. watch TV — watch TV

C Circle the correct word for each sentence.

1. I have lunch in the (**morning, afternoon**).

2. I have dinner in the (**morning, evening**).

3. I get up (**at, in**) 7 o'clock.

4. I go to bed (**at, in**) night.

Choose and write.

in　　on　　at　　at

1. What do you usually do __**on**__ Monday?
   I go to school.

2. What do you usually do ______ the morning?
   I have breakfast.

3. What do you usually do ______ night?
   I watch TV.

4. What time do you usually get up in the morning?
   I get up ______ 8 o'clock.

DAILY TEST

In and On

A Read and write.

1. 

in spring

in spring

2. 

in summer

in summer

3. 

in fall

in fall

4. 

in winter

in winter

B Match and write.

1. special days — special days
2. on Christmas — on Christmas
3. on New Year's Day — on New Year's Day
4. on my birthday — on my birthday

5. have a party — have a party

6. go hiking — go hiking

C Circle the correct word for each sentence.

1. I go hiking (**in**, **on**) spring.
2. I read books (**in, on**) fall.

3. I have a party (**in, on**) my birthday.
4. I go to church (**in, on**) Christmas.

D Choose and write.

have a party | go to the beach | go to the ski resort | have a big meal

1. What do you usually do in summer?
   I ___go to the beach___.

2. What do you usually do in winter?
   I ______________________.

3. What do people usually do on their birthdays?
   They ______________________.

4. What do people usually do on New Year's Day?
   They ______________________.

Textbook Answers and Translations

課本解答與翻譯

UNIT
1
A Cat In the Box 一隻貓在箱子裡
Prepositions of Location 表示地點的介系詞
Key Words 關鍵字彙
in
在……裡面
on
在……上面
under
在……下面
by
在……旁邊
box
盒子
basket
籃子
table
桌子
chair
椅子
Unit 1
A Cat In the Box
6
7

Match Up 連連看
將圖片連接到正確的單字。
in
在……裡面
on
在……上面
under
在……下面
by
在……旁邊
box
箱子
basket
籃子
table
桌子
chair
椅子
In or On? 在裡面？在上面？
圈出每個句子中正確的單字。
There is a dog (in, on) the box.
有一隻狗在箱子（裡面；上面）。
There is a cat (in, on) the box.
有一隻貓在箱子（裡面；上面）。
There is a dog (in, on) the basket.
有一隻狗在籃子（裡面；上面）。
There is a cat (in, on) the table.
有一隻貓在桌子（裡面；上面）。
Unit 1
A Cat In the Box
8
9

04
Under or By? 在下面？在旁邊？
圈出每個句子中正確的單字。
The cat is (under, by) the table.
貓在桌子（下面；旁邊）。
The cat is (under, by) the table.
貓在桌子（下面；旁邊）。
The dog is (under, by) the chair.
狗在椅子（下面；旁邊）。
The dog is (under, by) the chair.
狗在椅子（下面；旁邊）。
10

05
Where Is It? 牠在哪裡？
在單字 It 底下畫線。
圈出每個句子中正確的單字。
Unit 1
A Cat In the Box
Where is the dog? 狗在哪裡?
It is (in, on) the table.
牠在桌子（裡面；上面）。
Where is the cat? 貓在哪裡?
It is (under, by) the dog.
牠在狗（下面；旁邊）。
Where is the dog? 狗在哪裡?
It is (in, on) the basket.
牠在籃子（裡面；上面）。
Where is the cat? 貓在哪裡?
It is (under, by) the chair.
牠在椅子（下面；旁邊）。
11

06
I Can Read 我會閱讀
閱讀故事，找出每一隻動物並圈出來。
Unit 1
A Cat In the Box
Where Are They?
牠們在哪裡？
I see a cat. It is on the box.
我看到一隻貓。牠在箱子上面。
I see a dog. It is on the box, too.
我看到一隻狗。牠也在箱子上面。
I see a cat. It is by the box.
我看到一隻貓。牠在箱子旁邊。
I see a dog. It is in the box.
我看到一隻狗。牠在箱子裡面。
12
13

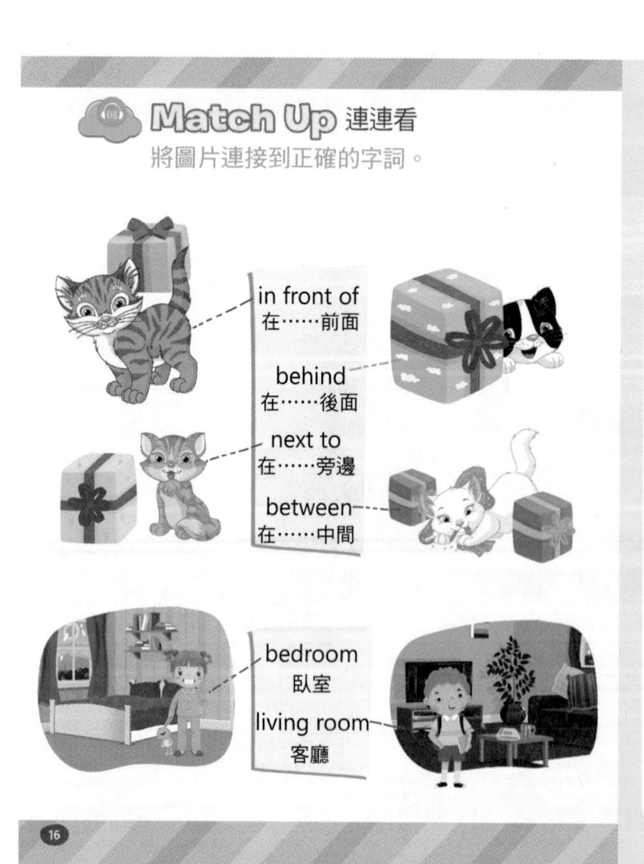

In Front Of or Behind? 在前面？在後面？

圈出每個句子中正確的字詞。

There is a sofa (in, **on**) the living room.
有一張沙發在客廳（裡面；上面）。

The sofa is (**in front of**, behind) the table.
沙發在桌子（前面；後面）。

The table is (in front of, **behind**) the sofa.
桌子在沙發（前面；後面）。

There is a TV (in front of, **behind**) the table.
電視在桌子（前面；後面）。

Unit 2 A Cat Next To the Box

17

在旁邊？在中間？

Next To or Between?

圈出每個句子中正確的字詞。

There is a bed (in, on) the bedroom.
有一張床在臥室（裡面；上面）。

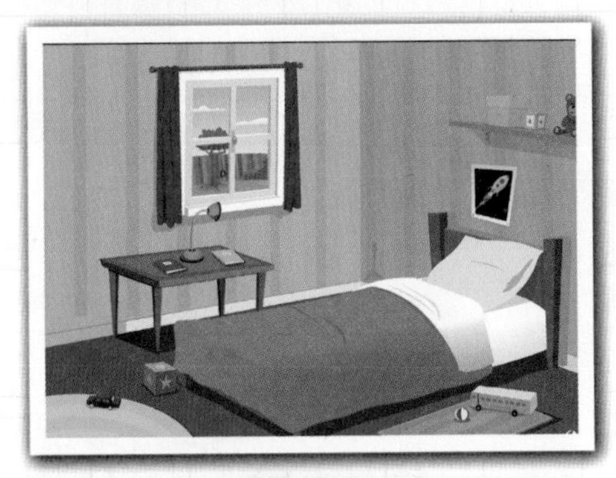

The bed is (next to, between) the table.
床在桌子（旁邊；中間）。

There is a lamp (in, on) the table.
檯燈在桌子（裡面；上面）。

There are books (in front of, next to) the lamp.
書本在檯燈（前面；旁邊）。

The lamp is (next to, between) the books.
檯燈在書本（旁邊；中間）。

它們在哪裡?

Where Are They?

在字詞 It 和 They 底下畫線。
圈出每個句子中正確的字詞。

Where is the sofa? 沙發在哪裡？
It is (next to, between) the two lamps.
它在兩座檯燈（旁邊；中間）。

Where are the lamps? 檯燈在哪裡？
They are (next to, between) the sofa.
它們在沙發（旁邊；中間）。

Where is the table? 桌子在哪裡？
It is (in front of, behind) the chairs.
它在椅子（前面；後面）。

Where are the chairs? 椅子在哪裡？
They are (in front of, behind) the table.
它們在桌子（前面；後面）。

I Can Read 我會閱讀

閱讀故事，並圈出每個句子中正確的字詞。

There is a desk (next to, between) the table.
There is a chair (in front of, behind) the desk.
On the desk, there is a computer.
有一張書桌在桌子（旁邊；中間）。
有一張椅子在書桌（前面；後面）。
在書桌上，有一台電腦。

There is a bed in my room.
There is a table (next to, between) the bed.
On the table, there is a lamp.
我的房間有一張床。有一張桌子在床（旁邊；中間）。
在桌子上，有一座檯燈。

What is between the bed and the desk?
The (table, chair) is between the bed and the desk.
什麼在床和書桌中間？
（桌子；椅子）在床和書桌中間。

UNIT
3
A Cat Below the Tree 一隻貓在樹下
Prepositions of Location 表示地點的介系詞
Unit 3 A Cat Below the Tree
Key Words 關鍵字彙
閱讀以下字詞。
above 在……上方
school 學校
below 在……下方
church 教堂
SCHOOL
beside 在……旁邊
POST OFFICE
Supermarket
supermarket
超市
post office
郵局
on the right 在右邊
on the left 在左邊
22
23

Match Up 連連看
將字詞連接到正確的圖片。
below 在……下方
above 在……上方
beside 在……旁邊
on the right
在右邊
on the left
在左邊
school 學校
church 教堂
post office
郵局
supermarket
超市
SUPERMARKET
24
在……下方？在……上方？
Below or Above?
圈出藍色的字詞。
Unit 3 A Cat Below the Tree
The bird is above the church.
The church is below the bird.
鳥在教堂的上方。
教堂在鳥的下方。
Elementary School
Post Office
The school is next to the post office.
The school is by the post office.
The school is beside the post office.
學校在郵局旁邊。
學校在郵局旁邊。
學校在郵局旁邊。
25

在右邊？在左邊？

圈出每個句子中正確的字詞。

Where Is Ann? 安在哪裡？

圈出每個句子中正確的字詞。

The school is (on the right, on the left) of the post office.
學校在郵局的（右邊；左邊）。

The post office is (on the right, on the left) of the school.
郵局在學校的（右邊；左邊）。

The church is (below, beside) the school.
教堂在學校的（下方；旁邊）。

The church is (between, beside) the school and the post office.
教堂在學校和郵局的（中間；旁邊）。

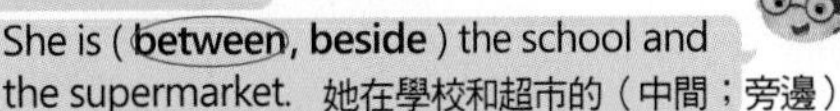

Where is Ann? 安在哪裡？
She is (between, beside) the school and the supermarket. 她在學校和超市的（中間；旁邊）。

Where is the school? 學校在哪裡？
It is (on the right, on the left) of Ann.
它在安的（右邊；左邊）。

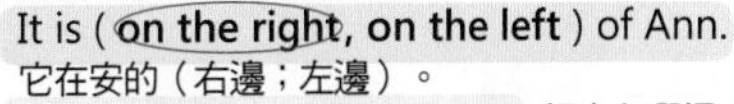

Where is the supermarket? 超市在哪裡？
It is (on the right, on the left) of Ann.
它在安的（右邊；左邊）。

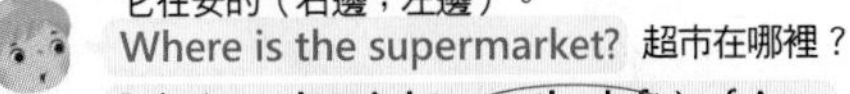

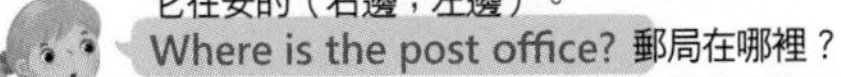

Where is the post office? 郵局在哪裡？
It is (between, beside) the supermarket.
它在超市的（中間；旁邊）。

I Can Read 我會閱讀

閱讀故事，並圈出藍色的字詞。

I live in a small town. 我住在一個小鎮。

There is a church beside my house.
The church is on the right of my house.
There is a post office on the right of the church.

有一座教堂在我家旁邊。
教堂在我家右邊。
有一間郵局在教堂右邊。

There is a supermarket next to my house.
The supermarket is on the left of my house.
There is a school on the left of the supermarket.

有一間超市在我家旁邊。
超市在我家左邊。
有一間學校在超市左邊。

There is a balloon above my house. 有一顆氣球在我家上方。
Can you find my house? 你可以找到我家嗎?

UNIT
4
Inside and Outside 在裡面和在外面
Prepositions of Location 表示地點的介系詞
19 Key Words 關鍵字彙
閱讀以下字詞。
inside
在……裡面
outside
在……外面
near
在……附近
far from
在……遠處
car
汽車
bus
公車
bus stop
公車站
BUS
30
31
Unit 4 Inside and Outside

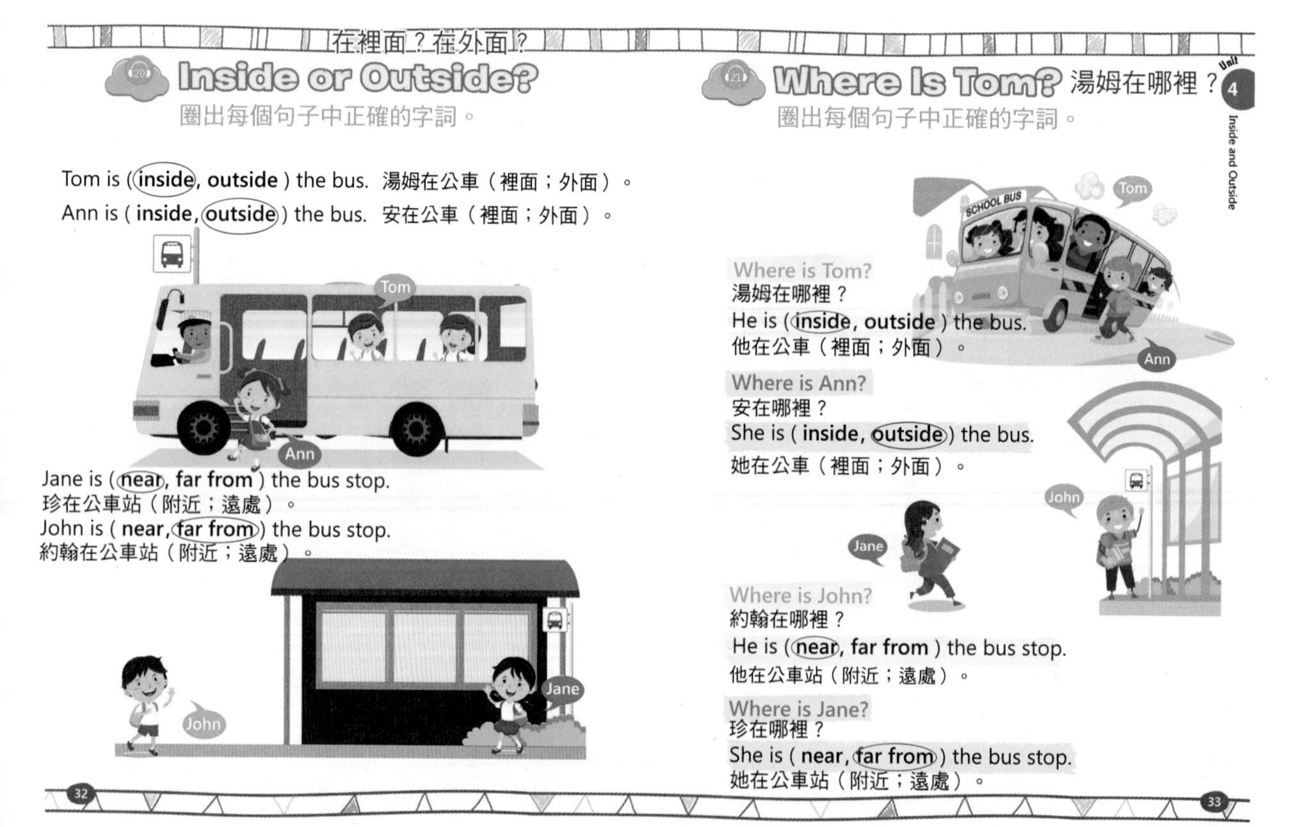
在裡面？在外面？
20 Inside or Outside?
圈出每個句子中正確的字詞。
Tom is (inside, outside) the bus. 湯姆在公車（裡面；外面）。
Ann is (inside, outside) the bus. 安在公車（裡面；外面）。
Tom
Ann
Jane is (near, far from) the bus stop.
珍在公車站（附近；遠處）。
John is (near, far from) the bus stop.
約翰在公車站（附近；遠處）。
John
Jane
21 Where Is Tom? 湯姆在哪裡？
圈出每個句子中正確的字詞。
SCHOOL BUS
Where is Tom?
湯姆在哪裡？
He is (inside, outside) the bus.
他在公車（裡面；外面）。
Where is Ann?
安在哪裡？
She is (inside, outside) the bus.
她在公車（裡面；外面）。
Where is John?
約翰在哪裡？
He is (near, far from) the bus stop.
他在公車站（附近；遠處）。
Where is Jane?
珍在哪裡？
She is (near, far from) the bus stop.
她在公車站（附近；遠處）。
32
33
Unit 4 Inside and Outside

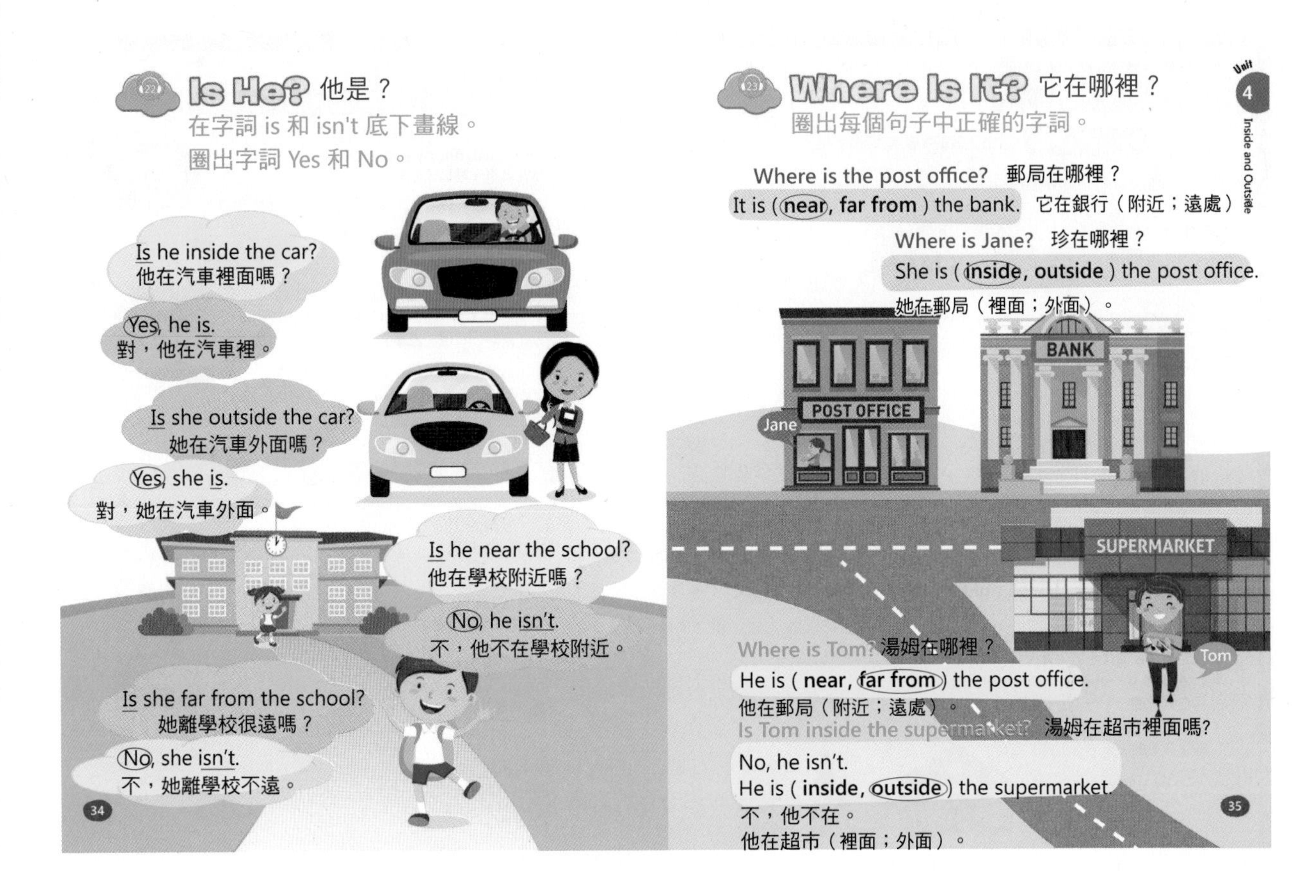
Is He? 他是？
在字詞 is 和 isn't 底下畫線。
圈出字詞 Yes 和 No。
Is he inside the car?
他在汽車裡面嗎？
Yes, he is.
對，他在汽車裡。
Is she outside the car?
她在汽車外面嗎？
Yes, she is.
對，她在汽車外面。
Is he near the school?
他在學校附近嗎？
No, he isn't.
不，他不在學校附近。
Is she far from the school?
她離學校很遠嗎？
No, she isn't.
不，她離學校不遠。
34
Where Is It? 它在哪裡？
圈出每個句子中正確的字詞。
Where is the post office? 郵局在哪裡？
It is (near, far from) the bank. 它在銀行（附近；遠處）
Where is Jane? 珍在哪裡？
She is (inside, outside) the post office.
她在郵局（裡面；外面）。
BANK
POST OFFICE
Jane
SUPERMARKET
Tom
Where is Tom? 湯姆在哪裡？
He is (near, far from) the post office.
他在郵局（附近；遠處）。
Is Tom inside the supermarket? 湯姆在超市裡面嗎?
No, he isn't.
He is (inside, outside) the supermarket.
不，他不在。
他在超市（裡面；外面）。
35
Unit 4 Inside and Outside

I Can Read 我會閱讀
閱讀故事，找出並連接朋友們。
Find the Friends.
尋找朋友們。
This is Jane.
She is near the bus stop.
這是珍。
她在公車站附近。
This is Ann.
She is far from the bus stop.
這是安。
她在公車站遠處。
This is Tom.
He is inside the car.
這是湯姆。
他在汽車裡。
This is Sam.
He is outside the car.
這是山姆。
他在汽車外面。
36
37
Unit 4 Inside and Outside

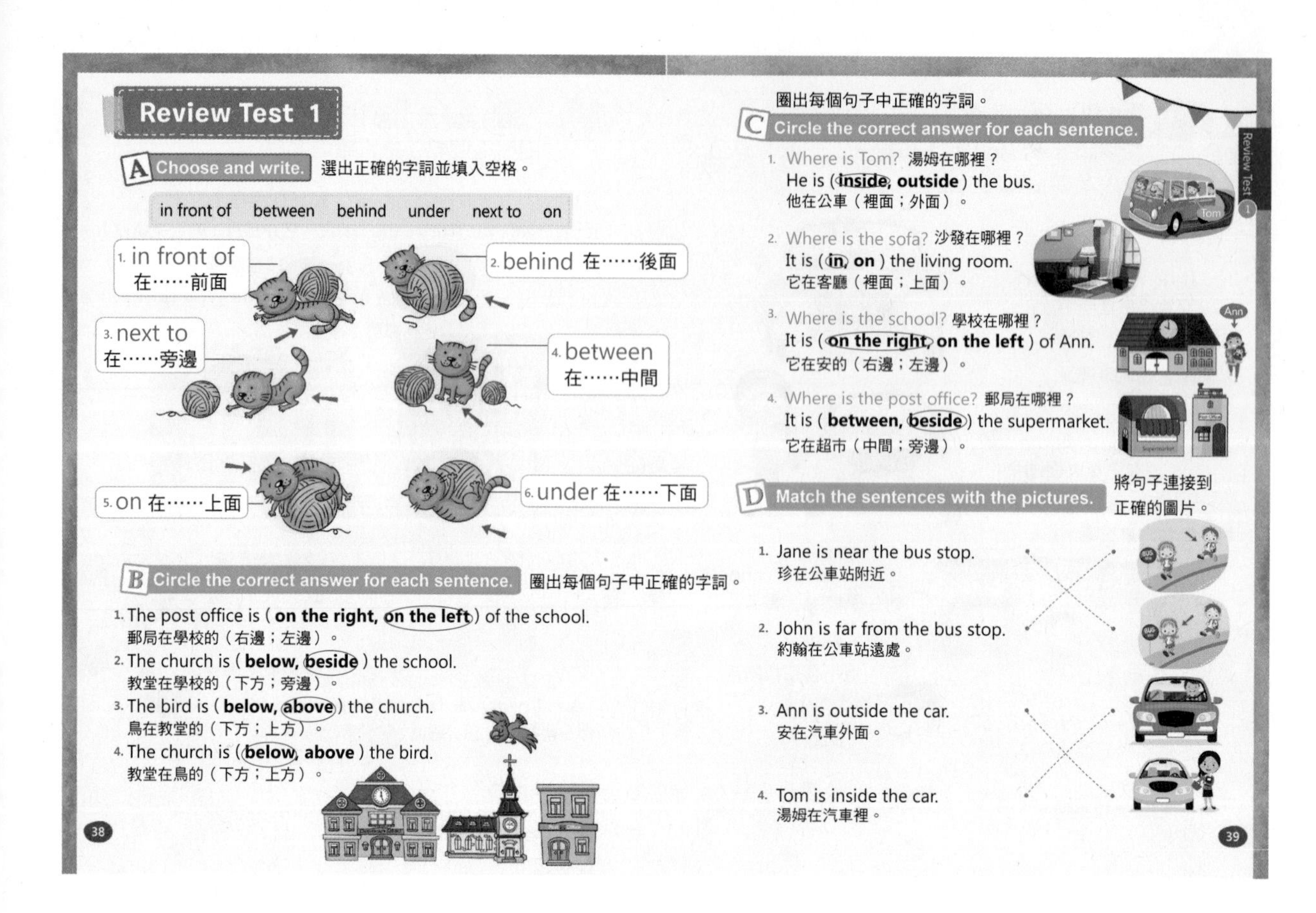

Review Test 1

A Choose and write. 選出正確的字詞並填入空格。

in front of　between　behind　under　next to　on

1. in front of 在……前面
2. behind 在……後面
3. next to 在……旁邊
4. between 在……中間
5. on 在……上面
6. under 在……下面

B Circle the correct answer for each sentence. 圈出每個句子中正確的字詞。

1. The post office is (**on the right, on the left**) of the school.
郵局在學校的（右邊；左邊）。
2. The church is (**below, beside**) the school.
教堂在學校的（下方；旁邊）。
3. The bird is (**below, above**) the church.
鳥在教堂的（下方；上方）。
4. The church is (**below, above**) the bird.
教堂在鳥的（下方；上方）。

38

C Circle the correct answer for each sentence. 圈出每個句子中正確的字詞。

1. Where is Tom? 湯姆在哪裡？
He is (**inside, outside**) the bus.
他在公車（裡面；外面）。
2. Where is the sofa? 沙發在哪裡？
It is (**in, on**) the living room.
它在客廳（裡面；上面）。
3. Where is the school? 學校在哪裡？
It is (**on the right, on the left**) of Ann.
它在安的（右邊；左邊）。
4. Where is the post office? 郵局在哪裡？
It is (**between, beside**) the supermarket.
它在超市（中間；旁邊）。

D Match the sentences with the pictures. 將句子連接到正確的圖片。

1. Jane is near the bus stop.
珍在公車站附近。
2. John is far from the bus stop.
約翰在公車站遠處。
3. Ann is outside the car.
安在汽車外面。
4. Tom is inside the car.
湯姆在汽車裡。

Review Test 1

39

UNIT 5

Up and Down 往上和往下

Prepositions of Direction and Movement
表示移動方向的介系詞

Key Words 關鍵字彙

閱讀以下字詞。

up 往上
down 往下
into 進去
out of 出來
stairs 階梯
elevator 電梯
pool 泳池
hill 山丘

Unit 5 Up and Down

40　41

往上？往下？

26 Up or Down?

圈出每個句子中正確的字詞。

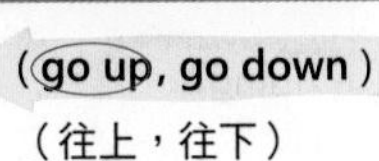

(go up, go down)
（往上，往下）

(go up, go down)
（往上，往下）

(go into, go out of)
（進去，出來）

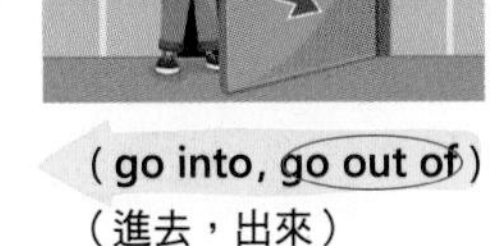

(go into, go out of)
（進去，出來）

往上？往下？

27 Go Up or Go Down?

圈出每個句子中正確的字詞。

He is going (up, **down**) the stairs.
他正在（上；下）樓梯。

She is going (**up**, down) the stairs.
她正在（上；下）樓梯。

The elevator is going (up, **down**).
電梯正在（上樓；下樓）。

The elevator is going (**up**, down).
電梯正在（上樓；下樓）。

The balloon is going (up, **down**).
氣球正在（上升；下降）。

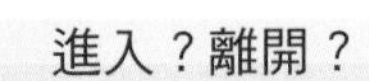

進入？離開？

28 Go Into or Go Out Of?

圈出每個句子中正確的字詞。

She is going (into, out of) the school.
她正（進入；離開）學校。
He is going (into, out of) the school.
他正（進入；離開）學校。

She is going (into, out of) the pool.
她正（進入；離開）泳池。
He is going (into, out of) the pool.
他正（進入；離開）泳池。

他正在做什麼？

29 What Is He Doing?

圈出有 ing的單字。

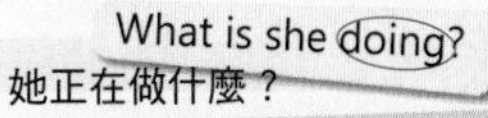

What is she doing?
她正在做什麼？
She is going up the stairs.
她正在上樓梯。

What is he doing? 他正在做什麼？
He is going down the stairs.
他正在下樓梯。

What is she doing?
她正在做什麼？
She is going into the pool.
她正進入泳池。

What is he doing? 他正在做什麼？
He is going out of the pool.
他正離開泳池。

I Can Read 我會閱讀
閱讀故事，並圈出藍色的字詞。
What is Ben doing?
班正在做什麼？
He is going up the hill.
他正在上山。
What is Tom doing?
湯姆正在做什麼？
He is going down the hill.
他正在下山。
What is Jane doing?
珍正在做什麼？
She is going into the water.
她正跳進水裡。
What is it doing?
牠正在做什麼？
It is going out of the water.
牠正跳出水面。
46
47
Unit 5 Up and Down

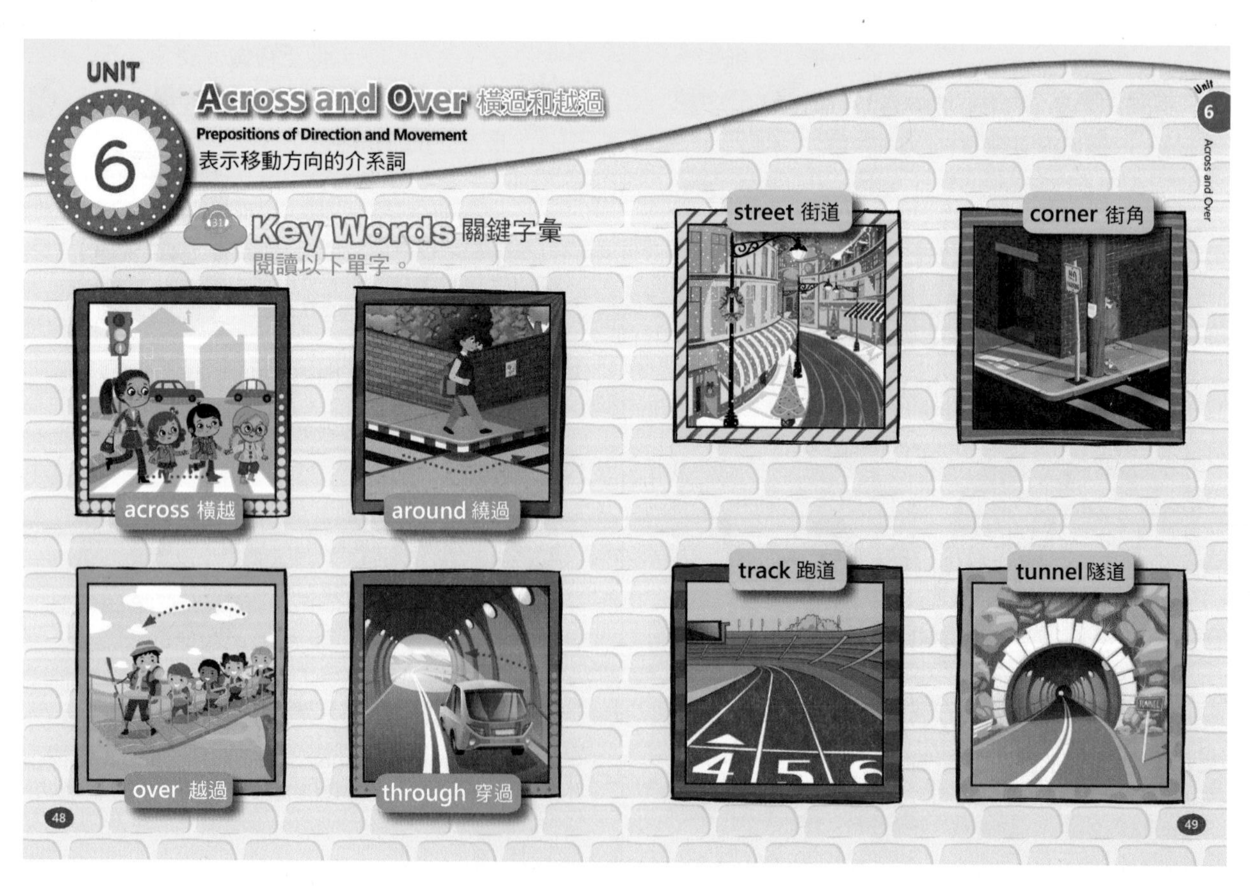
UNIT 6
Across and Over 橫過和越過
Prepositions of Direction and Movement
表示移動方向的介系詞
Key Words 關鍵字彙
閱讀以下單字。
across 橫越
around 繞過
over 越過
through 穿過
street 街道
corner 街角
track 跑道
tunnel 隧道
48
49
Unit 6 Across and Over

32 Across or Around? 橫越？繞過？

圈出每張圖片中正確的字詞。

(go across, go around)
（橫越，繞過）

(go across, go around)
（橫越，繞過）

(go over, go through)
（越過，穿過）

(go over, go through)
（越過，穿過）

50

33 Go Across or Go Around? 橫越？繞過？

圈出每個句子中正確的字詞。

She is going (across, around) the street.
她正（橫越；繞過）街道。

He is going (across, around) the corner.
他正（橫越；繞過）街角。

They are going (across, around) the street.
他們正（橫越；繞過）街道。

They are going (across, around) the track.
他們正（橫越；繞過）跑道。

Unit 6 Across and Over

51

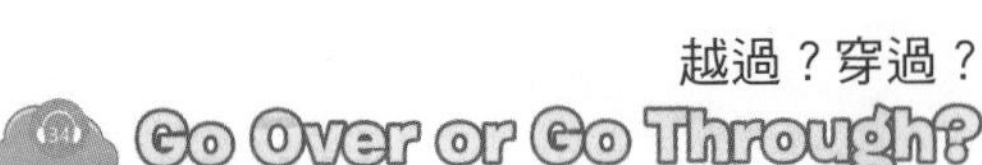

34 Go Over or Go Through? 越過？穿過？

圈出每個句子中正確的字詞。

He is going (over, through) the bar.
他正（越過；穿過）欄杆。

The bus is going (over, through) the gate.
公車正（越過；穿過）大門。

The cars are going (over, through) the bridge.
車子正（越過；穿過）橋樑。

The train is going (over, through) the tunnel.
火車正（越過；穿過）隧道。

52

35 What Is Ben Doing? 班正在做什麼？

在字詞 What is 底下畫線。
圈出每個句子中正確的字詞。

Ben

Tom

What is Ben doing? 班正在做什麼？
He is going (around, over) the track. 他正（繞過；越過）小徑。

What is Tom doing? 湯姆正在做什麼？
He is going (around, over) the bar.
他正（繞過；越過）欄杆。

What is Ann doing? 安正在做什麼？
She is going (through , around) the finish line.
她正（穿過；繞過）終點線。

Ann

What is Jane doing? 珍正在做什麼？
She is going (across, over) the street.
她正（橫越；越過）街道。

Jane

Unit 6 Across and Over

53

I Can Read 我會閱讀
閱讀故事，並圈出藍色的字詞。
What are they doing? 他們正在做什麼?
They are going through the finish line.
他們正穿過終點線。
What are they doing? 他們正在做什麼?
They are going around the corner.
他們正繞過轉角。
What are they doing? 他們正在做什麼?
They are going across the snow field.
他們正橫越雪原。
What are the cars doing?
車子正在做什麼?
They are going over the bridge.
他們正越過橋樑。
195
WEST
Unit 6
Across and Over
54
55

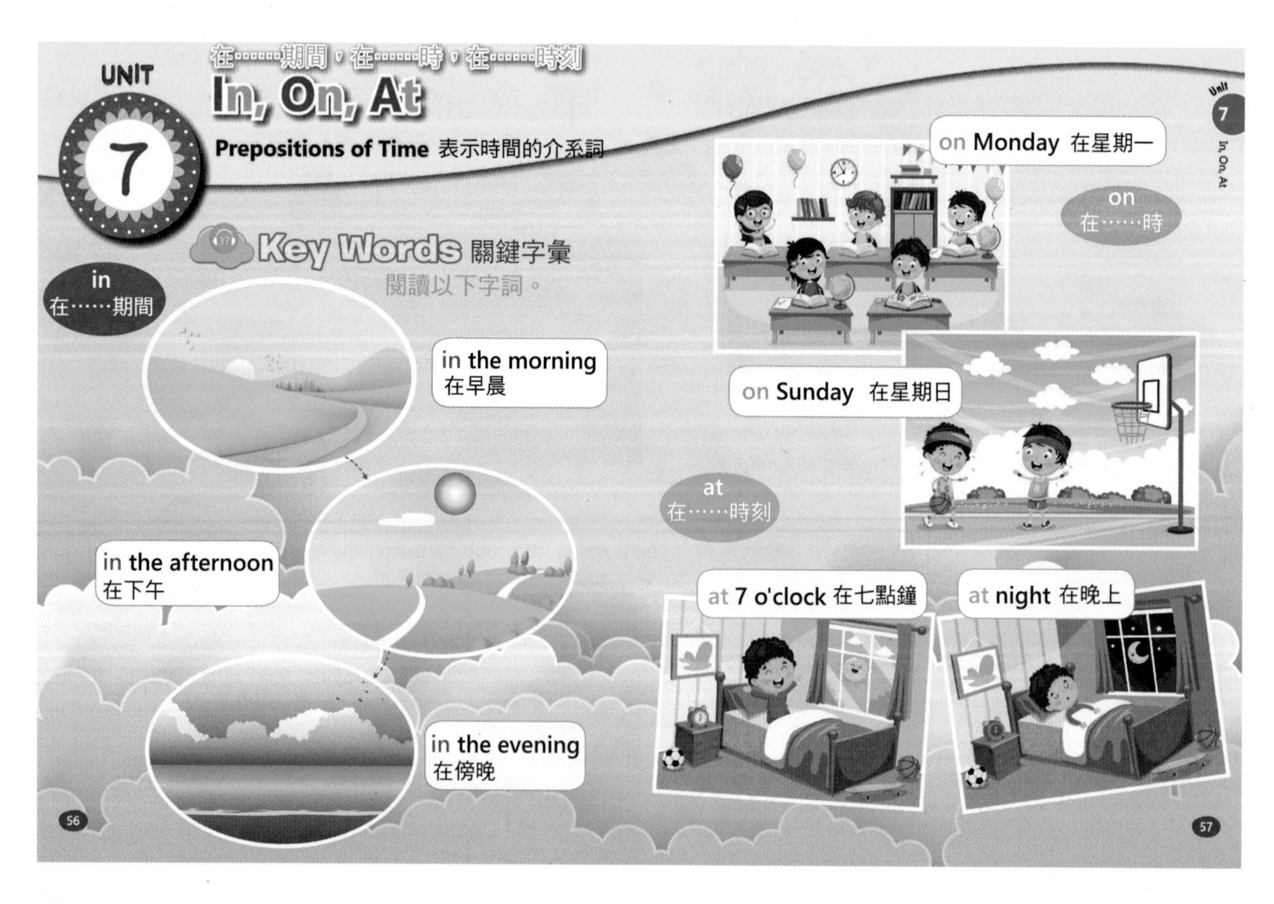
UNIT 7
在……期間，在……時，在……時刻
In, On, At
Prepositions of Time 表示時間的介系詞
Key Words 關鍵字彙
閱讀以下字詞。
in
在……期間
in the morning
在早晨
in the afternoon
在下午
in the evening
在傍晚
on
在……時
on Monday 在星期一
on Sunday 在星期日
at
在……時刻
at 7 o'clock 在七點鐘
at night 在晚上
Unit 7
In, On, At
56
57

Match Up 連連看

將字詞連接到正確的圖片。

get up
起床
have breakfast
吃早餐

have lunch
吃午餐
have dinner
吃晚餐

go to school
上學
go to church
上教堂

go to bed
上床睡覺
watch TV
看電視

In the Morning 在早上

圈出每個句子中正確的單字。

I have breakfast in the (morning, afternoon).
我在（早上；下午）吃早餐。

I have lunch in the (morning, afternoon).
我在（早上；下午）吃午餐。

I have dinner in the (morning, evening).
我在（早上；傍晚）吃晚餐。

I go to bed at (night, morning).
我在（晚上；早上）上床睡覺。

I Do 我做……

圈出每個句子中正確的單字。

I go to school (on, in) Monday.
我（在；在）星期一上學。

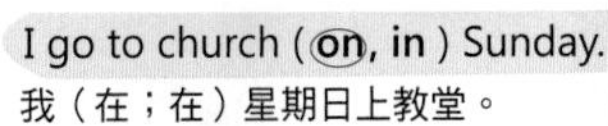

I go to church (on, in) Sunday.
我（在；在）星期日上教堂。

I have lunch (on, in) the afternoon.
我（在；在）下午吃午餐。

I get up (at, in) 7 o'clock.
我（在；在）七點鐘起床。

I go to bed (at, in) night.
我（在；在）晚上上床睡覺。

What Do You Usually Do? 你通常做什麼？

在字詞 What do you usually do 底下畫線。
將句子連接到正確的圖片。

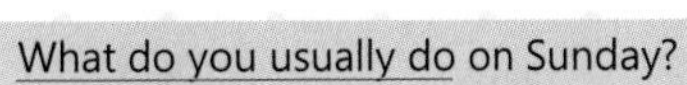

What do you usually do on Monday?
你星期一通常做什麼？

I go to school.
我上學去。

What do you usually do on Sunday?
你星期日通常做什麼？

I go to church.
我上教堂。

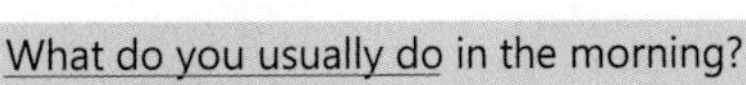

What do you usually do in the morning?
你早上通常做什麼？

I have breakfast.
我吃早餐。

What do you usually do at night?
你晚上通常做什麼？

I watch TV.
我看電視。

I Can Read 我會閱讀
閱讀故事，並將每組句子連接到正確的圖片。
Day and Night 白天和晚上
It is day.
The sun shines during the day.
We go to school during the day.
現在是白天。
整天都陽光普照。
我們在白天去上學。
It is night.
The moon shines at night.
We go to bed at night.
現在是晚上。
月亮在晚上閃耀。
我們在晚上上床睡覺。
Unit 7
In, On, At
62
63

UNIT 8
In and On 在……期間，在……特定日
Prepositions of Time
表示時間的介系詞
Key Words 關鍵字彙
閱讀以下字詞。
in spring 在春天
in summer 在夏天
Seasons
季節
in fall 在秋天
in winter 在冬天
Special Days
特別日
MERRY CHRISTMAS!
on Christmas 在聖誕節
on New Year's Day
在元旦
HAPPY BIRTHDAY
on my birthday
在我的生日
Unit 8
In and On
64
65

Match Up 連連看

將字詞連接到正確的圖片。

go to the beach
去海灘

go to the ski resort
去滑雪場

go hiking
去健行

have a party
舉辦派對

have a big meal
吃大餐

read a book
閱讀書籍

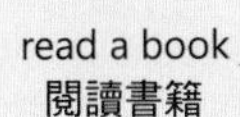

In Summer 在夏天

圈出每個句子中正確的單字。

I go hiking (in, on) spring. 我（在；在）春天去健行。

I go to the beach (in, on) summer. 我（在；在）夏天去海灘。

I go to the ski resort (in, on) winter. 我（在；在）冬天去滑雪場。

I have a party (in, on) my birthday.
我（在；在）生日舉辦派對。

We have a big meal (in, on) New Year's Day.
我們（在；在）元旦吃大餐。

We go to church (in, on) Christmas.
我們（在；在）聖誕節上教堂。

你通常做什麼？

What Do You Usually Do?

圈出每個句子中正確的單字。
將句子連接到正確的圖片。

What do you usually do (in, on) spring?
你通常（在；在）春天做什麼？
I go hiking. 我去健行。

What do you usually do (in, on) summer?
你通常（在；在）夏天做什麼？
I go to the beach. 我去海灘。

What do you usually do (in, on) fall?
你通常（在；在）秋天做什麼？
I read books. 我閱讀書籍。

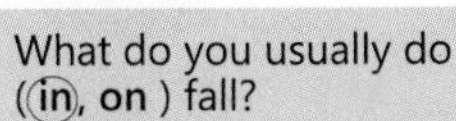

What do you usually do (in, on) winter?
你通常(在；在)冬天做什麼？
I go to the ski resort.
我去滑雪場。

人們通常做什麼？

What Do People Usually Do?

圈出每個句子中正確的單字。
在單字 They 底下畫線。

What do people usually do (in, on) their birthdays?
人們通常（在；在）生日時做什麼？
They have a party. 他們舉辦派對。

What do people usually do (in, on) New Year's Day?
人們通常（在；在）元旦時做什麼？
They have a big meal. 他們吃大餐。

What do people usually do (in, on) summer?
人們通常（在；在）夏天做什麼？
They go to the beach. 他們去海灘。

What do people usually do (in, on) winter?
人們通常（在；在）冬天做什麼？
They go to the ski resort. 他們去滑雪場。

I Can Read 我會閱讀
閱讀故事，
並勾選出句子是否與圖片相符。
What Do People Usually Do?
人們通常做什麼？
People usually go to the ski resort in winter.
人們通常在冬天去滑雪場。
Yes No
People usually go to the beach in summer.
人們通常在夏天去海灘。
Yes No
People usually have a party on their birthdays.
人們通常在生日時舉辦派對。
Yes No
People usually have a big meal on New Year's Day.
人們通常在元旦吃大餐。
Yes No
70
71

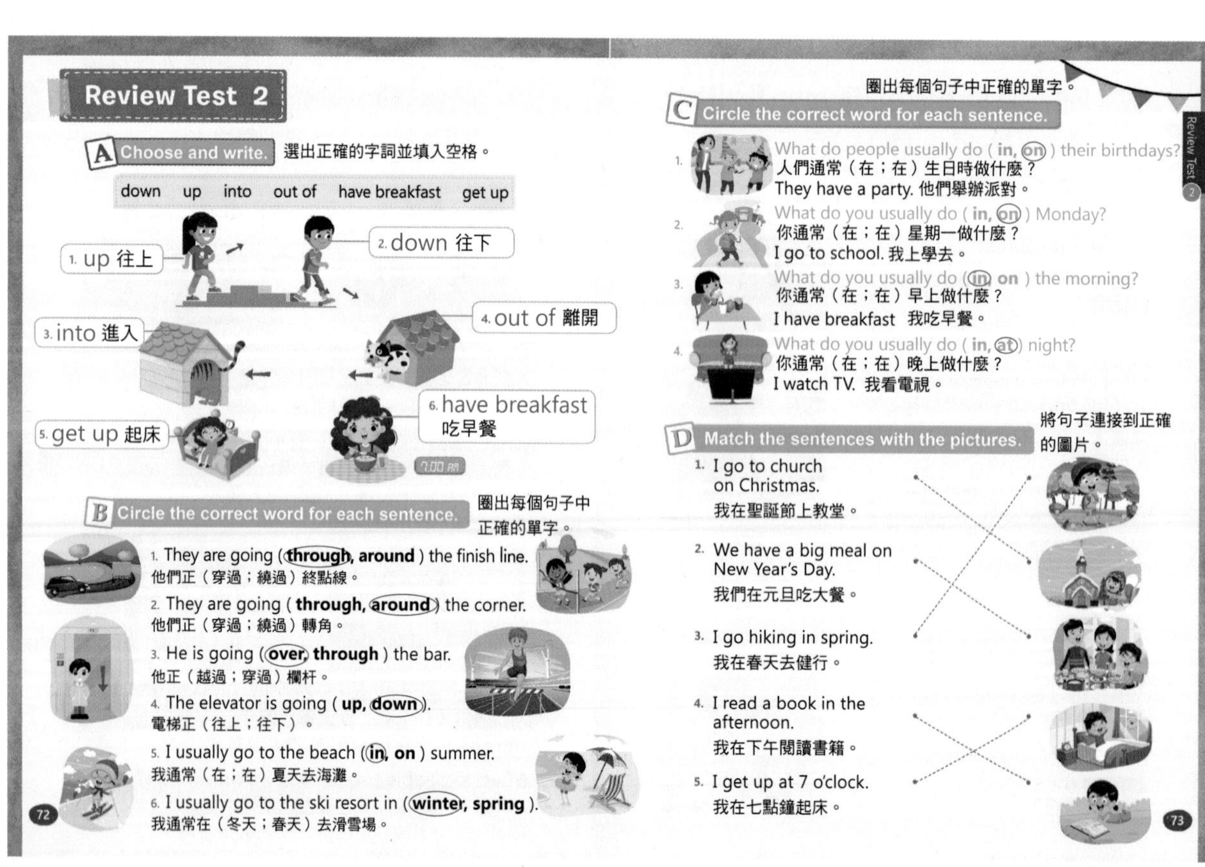
Review Test 2
A Choose and write. 選出正確的字詞並填入空格。
down up into out of have breakfast get up
1. up 往上
2. down 往下
3. into 進入
4. out of 離開
5. get up 起床
6. have breakfast 吃早餐
B Circle the correct word for each sentence. 圈出每個句子中正確的單字。
1. They are going (through, around) the finish line.
他們正（穿過；繞過）終點線。
2. They are going (through, around) the corner.
他們正（穿過；繞過）轉角。
3. He is going (over, through) the bar.
他正（越過；穿過）欄杆。
4. The elevator is going (up, down).
電梯正（往上；往下）。
5. I usually go to the beach (in, on) summer.
我通常（在；在）夏天去海灘。
6. I usually go to the ski resort in (winter, spring).
我通常在（冬天；春天）去滑雪場。
C Circle the correct word for each sentence. 圈出每個句子中正確的單字。
1. What do people usually do (in, on) their birthdays?
人們通常（在；在）生日時做什麼？
They have a party. 他們舉辦派對。
2. What do you usually do (in, on) Monday?
你通常（在；在）星期一做什麼？
I go to school. 我上學去。
3. What do you usually do (in, on) the morning?
你通常（在；在）早上做什麼？
I have breakfast 我吃早餐。
4. What do you usually do (in, at) night?
你通常（在；在）晚上做什麼？
I watch TV. 我看電視。
D Match the sentences with the pictures. 將句子連接到正確的圖片。
1. I go to church on Christmas.
我在聖誕節上教堂。
2. We have a big meal on New Year's Day.
我們在元旦吃大餐。
3. I go hiking in spring.
我在春天去健行。
4. I read a book in the afternoon.
我在下午閱讀書籍。
5. I get up at 7 o'clock.
我在七點鐘起床。
72
73

Daily Test Answers

課堂練習解答

DAILY TEST 1

A Cat In the Box

A Read and write.

1. box — box

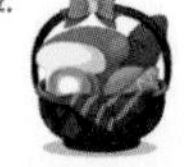
2. basket — basket

3. table — table

4. chair — chair

B Match and write.

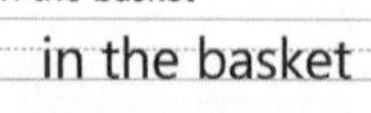
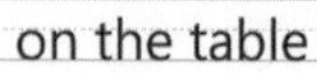

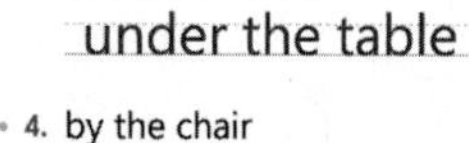
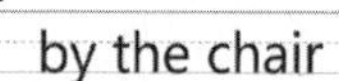

1. in the basket — in the basket
2. on the table — on the table
3. under the table — under the table
4. by the chair — by the chair

C Circle the correct word for each sentence.

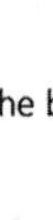
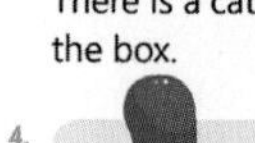
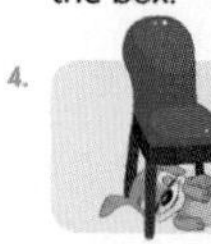

1. There is a cat (in, on) the box. [in circled]
2. There is a cat (in, on) the box. [on circled]
3. The dog is (by, under) the chair. [by circled]
4. The dog is (by, under) the chair. [under circled]

D Choose and write.

by   on   in   under

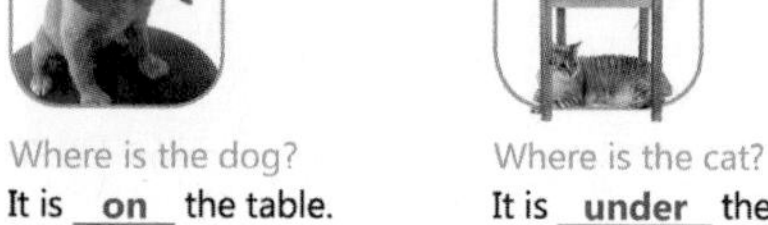

1. Where is the cat?
   It is __by__ the dog.
2. Where is the dog?
   It is __in__ the basket.
3. Where is the dog?
   It is __on__ the table.
4. Where is the cat?
   It is __under__ the chair.

DAILY TEST 2

A Cat Next To the Box

A Read and write.

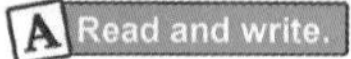
1. in front of — in front of
2. behind — behind

3. next to — next to
4. between — between

B Match and write.

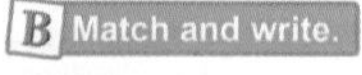

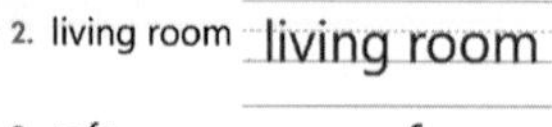
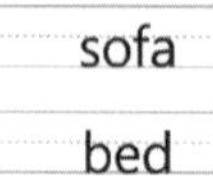

1. bedroom — bedroom
2. living room — living room
3. sofa — sofa
4. bed — bed
5. lamp — lamp
6. TV — TV

C Circle the correct word or words for each sentence.

1. The sofa is (in front of, behind) the table. [behind circled]
2. The table is (in front of, behind) the sofa. [in front of circled]
3. The sofa is (next to, between) the two lamps. [between circled]
4. The lamps are (next to, between) the sofa. [next to circled]

D Choose and write.

between   behind   in front of   next to

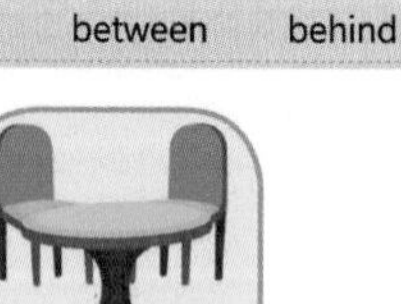
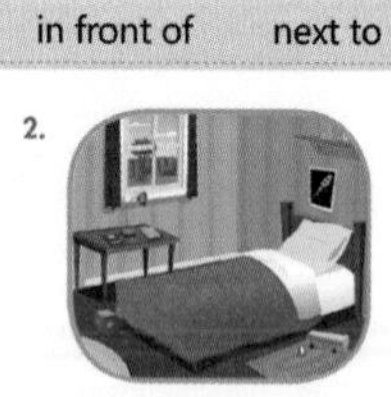
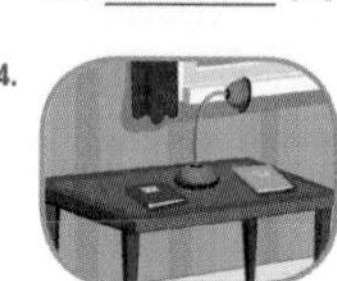

1. Where are the chairs?
   They are __behind__ the table.
2. Where is the table?
   It is __next to__ the bed.
3. Where is the chair?
   It is __in front of__ the desk.
4. Where is the lamp?
   It is __between__ the two books.

DAILY TEST 3

A Cat Below the Tree

A Read and write.

1. 
below
below

2. 
above
above

3. 
beside
beside

4. 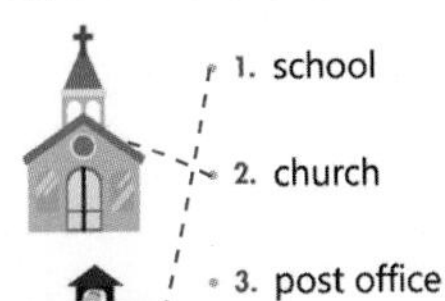
on the right
on the right

5. 
on the left
on the left

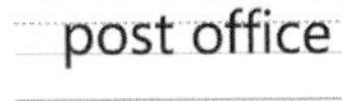

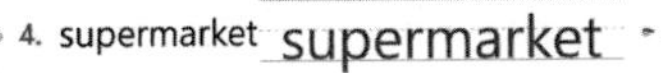

B Match and write.

1. school — school
2. church — church
3. post office — post office
4. supermarket — supermarket

C Circle the correct word or words for each sentence.

1. The bird is (**below, above**) the church.
2. The church is (**below, above**) the bird.
3. The school is (**on the right, on the left**) of Ann.
4. The church is (**below, beside**) the school.

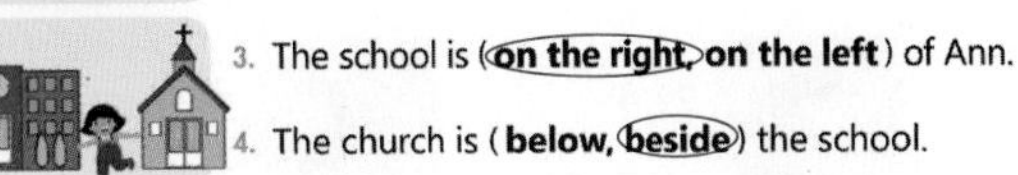

D Choose and write.

beside above on the left on the right

1. Where is the church?
It is beside the house.
2. Where is the supermarket?
It is on the left of the house.
3. Where is the post office?
It is on the right of the church.
4. Where is the balloon?
It is above the house.

DAILY TEST 4

Inside and Outside

A Read and write.

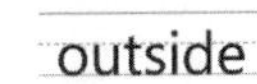
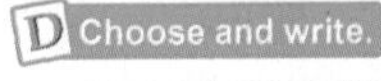

1. inside
inside

2. outside
outside

3. near
near

4. far from
far from

B Match and write.

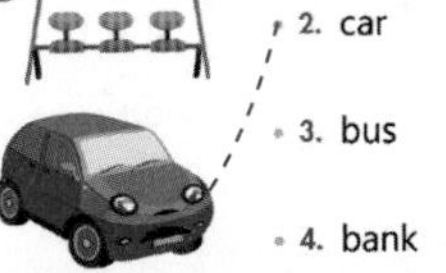

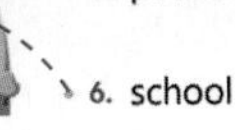
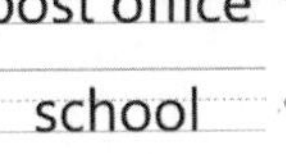

1. bus stop — bus stop
2. car — car
3. bus — bus
4. bank — bank
5. post office — post office
6. school — school

C Circle the correct word or words for each sentence.

1. Tom is (**inside, outside**) the bus.
2. Ann is (**inside, outside**) the bus.
3. John is (**near, far from**) the bus stop.
4. Jane is (**near, far from**) the bus stop.

D Choose and write.

inside outside near far from

1. Is he inside the car?
Yes, he is.
2. Is she outside the car?
Yes, she is.
3. Where is the post office?
It is near the bank.
4. Where is Tom?
He is far from the post office.

DAILY TEST 5

Up and Down

A Read and write.

1.  go up — go up
2.  go down — go down
3. go into — go into
4.  go out of — go out of

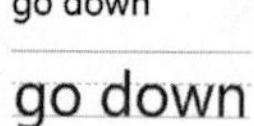

B Match and write.

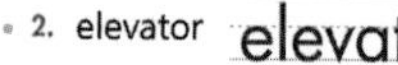

1. stairs — stairs
2. elevator — elevator
3. pool — pool
4. hill — hill

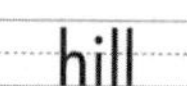

C Circle the correct word or words for each sentence.

1.  Ben is going (**up**, down) the hill.
2.  Tom is going (up, **down**) the hill.
3.  Jane is going (**into**, out of) the pool.
4.  Sam is going (into, **out of**) the pool.

D Choose and write.

going down going up going into going out of

1.  What is he doing? He is going up the stairs.
2.  What is she doing? She is going down the stairs.
3.  What is she doing? She is going into the water.
4.  What is it doing? It is going out of the water.

DAILY TEST 6

Across and Over

A Read and write.

1.  go across — go across
2.  go around — go around
3.  go over — go over
4.  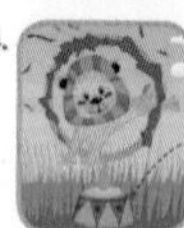 go through — go through

B Match and write.

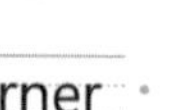

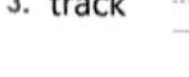

1. street — street
2. corner — corner
3. track — track
4. tunnel — tunnel
5. gate — gate

C Circle the correct word for each sentence.

1.  Jane is going (**across**, around) the street.
2.  Tom is going (across, **around**) the corner.
3.  He is going (**over**, through) the bar.
4.  The bus is going (over, **through**) the gate.

D Choose and write.

going around going across going over going through

1.  What is he doing? ⇨He is going around the track.
2.  What is she doing? ⇨She is going through the finish line.
3.   What are they doing? ⇨They are going across the street.
4.  What are the cars doing? ⇨They are going over the bridge.

DAILY TEST 7

In, On, At

A Read and write.

1. 
in the morning
in the morning

2. 
in the afternoon
in the afternoon

3. 
in the evening
in the evening

4. 
at night
at night

B Match and write.

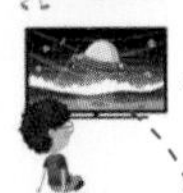

1. get up — get up
2. have breakfast — have breakfast
3. go to school — go to school
4. go to church — go to church
5. go to bed — go to bed
6. watch TV — watch TV

C Circle the correct word for each sentence.

1. I have lunch in the (**morning**, **afternoon**).
2. I have dinner in the (**morning**, **evening**).
3. I get up (**at**, **in**) 7 o'clock.
4. I go to bed (**at**, **in**) night.

D Choose and write.

in on at at

1. What do you usually do __on__ Monday?
I go to school.

2. What do you usually do __in__ the morning?
I have breakfast.

3. What do you usually do __at__ night?
I watch TV.

4. What time do you usually get up in the morning?
I get up __at__ 8 o'clock.

DAILY TEST 8

In and On

A Read and write.

1. 
in spring
in spring

2. 
in summer
in summer

3. 
in fall
in fall

4. 
in winter
in winter

B Match and write.

1. special days — special days
2. on Christmas — on Christmas
3. on New Year's Day — on New Year's Day
4. on my birthday — on my birthday
5. have a party — have a party
6. go hiking — go hiking

C Circle the correct word for each sentence.

1. I go hiking (**in**, **on**) spring.
2. I read books (**in**, **on**) fall.
3. I have a party (**in**, **on**) my birthday.
4. I go to church (**in**, **on**) Christmas.

D Choose and write.

have a party go to the beach go to the ski resort have a big meal

1. What do you usually do in summer?
I __go to the beach__.

2. What do you usually do in winter?
I __go to the ski resort__.

3. What do people usually do on their birthdays?
They __have a party__.

4. What do people usually do on New Year's Day?
They __have a big meal__.

The Best Preparation for Building Basic Vocabulary and Grammar

The Reading Key — Preschool series is designed to help children understand basic words and grammar to learn English. This series also helps children develop their reading skills in a fun and easy way.

Features

- Learning high-frequency words that appear in all kinds of reading material
- Building basic grammar and reading comprehension skills to learn English
- Various activities including reading and writing practice
- A wide variety of topics that cover American school subjects
- Full-color photographs and illustrations

The Reading Key series has five levels.

- Reading Key **Preschool 1–6**
  a six-book series designed for preschoolers and kindergarteners
- Reading Key **Basic 1–4**
  a four-book series designed for kindergarteners and beginners
- Reading Key **Volume 1–3**
  a three-book series designed for beginner to intermediate learners
- Reading Key **Volume 4–6**
  a three-book series designed for intermediate to high-intermediate learners
- Reading Key **Volume 7–9**
  a three-book series designed for high-intermediate learners

Table of Contents | Preschool 4 Prepositions

Components Workbook for Daily Review • Answers and Translations

Syllabus | Preschool 4 Prepositions

Subject	Unit	Grammar	Vocabulary
Prepositions & Usage	Unit 1 A Cat In the Box	Prepositions of Location 1	• in, on, under, by • box, basket • table, chair
	Unit 2 A Cat Next To the Box	Prepositions of Location 2	• in front of, behind • next to, between • bedroom, living room • bed, lamp, sofa, table, TV
	Unit 3 A Cat Below the Tree	Prepositions of Location 3	• below, above, beside • on the right, on the left • school, church, post office, supermarket
	Unit 4 Inside and Outside	Prepositions of Location 4	• inside, outside • near, far from • bus stop, car, bus
	Unit 5 Up and Down	Prepositions of Direction and Movement 1	• up, down, into, out of • go up, go down, go into, go out of • stairs, elevator, pool, hill
	Unit 6 Across and Over	Prepositions of Direction and Movement 2	• across, around, over, through • go across, go around, go over, go through • street, corner, track, tunnel
	Unit 7 In, On, At	Prepositions of Time 1	• in the morning, in the afternoon, in the evening • on Monday, on Sunday • at 7 o'clock, at night • get up, have breakfast, go to school, go to church, go to bed, watch TV
	Unit 8 In and On	Prepositions of Time 2	• seasons: in spring, in summer, in fall, in winter • special days: on Christmas, on New Year's Day, on one's birthday • go to the beach, go to the ski resort, go hiking, have a party, have a big meal

UNIT
1
A Cat In the Box
Prepositions of Location
01
Key Words Read the words.
in
on
under
by

basket

box

table

chair

Match the words with the pictures.

Circle the correct word for each sentence.

There is a dog (**in**, **on**) the box.

There is a cat (**in**, **on**) the box.

There is a dog (**in**, **on**) the basket.

There is a cat (**in**, **on**) the table.

Under or By?

Circle the correct word for each sentence.

The cat is (under, by) the table.

The cat is (**under, by**) the table.

The dog is (**under, by**) the chair.

Where Is It?

Underline the word **It**. Circle the correct word for each sentence.

Where is the dog?
It is (**in**, **on**) the table.

Where is the cat?
It is (**under**, **by**) the dog.

Where is the dog?
It is (**in**, **on**) the basket.

Where is the cat?
It is (**under**, **by**) the chair.

I Can Read

Read the story.
Find each animal and circle it.

Where Are They?

I see a cat. It is on the box.

I see a dog. It is on the box, too.

I see a cat. It is by the box.
I see a dog. It is in the box.

A Cat Next To the Box

Prepositions of Location

Key Words Read the words.

living room

between

next to

Match the words with the pictures.

in front of

behind

next to

between

bedroom

living room

In Front Of or Behind?

Circle the correct answer for each sentence.

There is a sofa (**in**, **on**) the living room.

The sofa is (**in front of**, **behind**) the table.

The table is (**in front of**, **behind**) the sofa.

There is a TV (**in front of**, **behind**) the table.

Next To or Between?

Circle the correct answer for each sentence.

There is a bed (**in**, **on**) the bedroom.

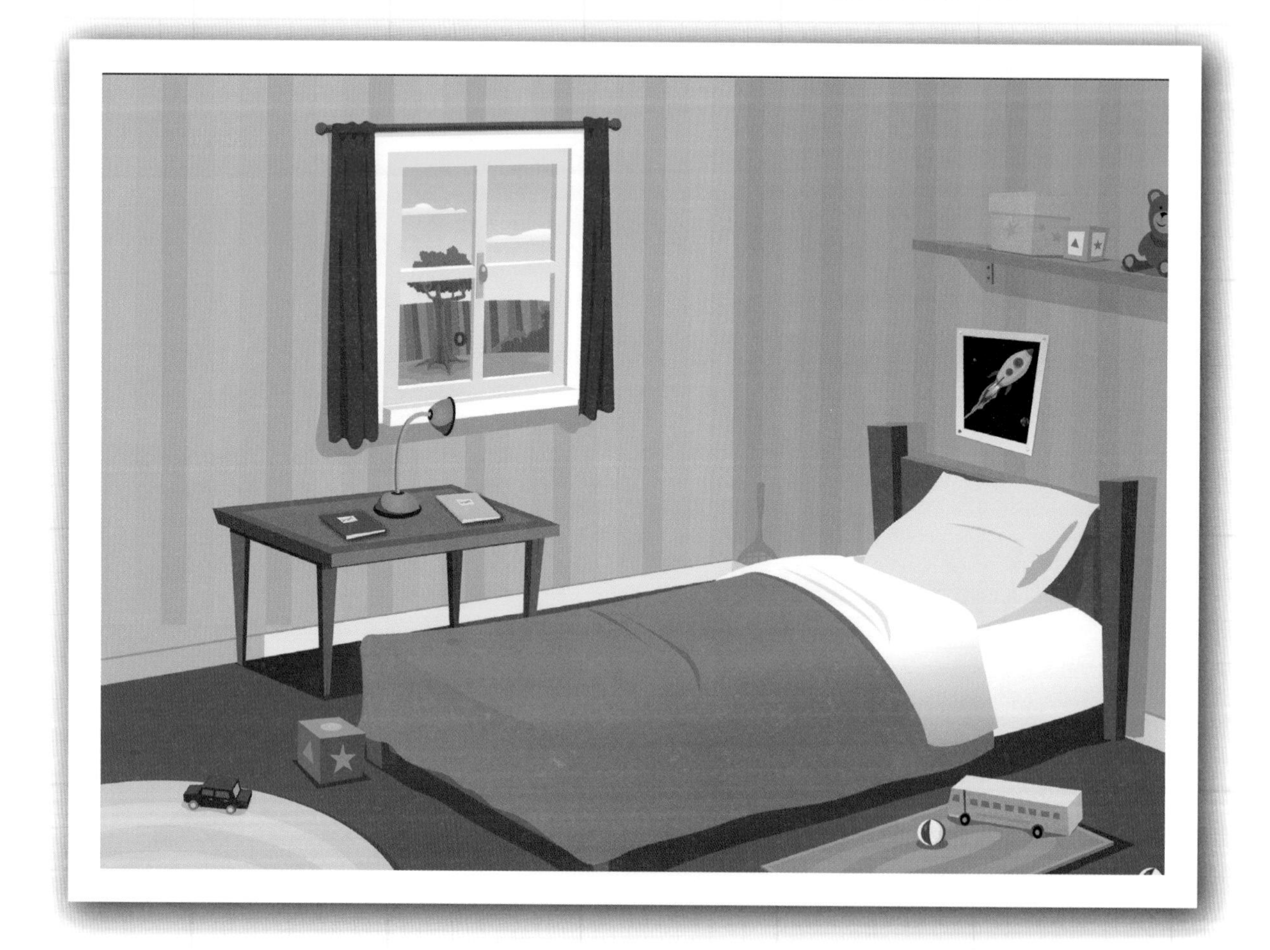

The bed is (**next to, between**) the table.

There is a lamp (**in, on**) the table.

There are books (**in front of, next to**) the lamp.

The lamp is (**next to, between**) the books.

Where Are They?

Underline the words **It** and **They**.

Circle the correct answer for each sentence.

Where is the sofa?

It is (**next to**, **between**) the two lamps.

Where are the lamps?

They are (**next to**, **between**) the sofa.

Where is the table?

It is (**in front of**, **behind**) the chairs.

Where are the chairs?

They are (**in front of**, **behind**) the table.

I Can Read

Read the story.

Circle the correct answer for each sentence.

There is a bed in my room.

There is a table (**next to**, **between**) the bed.

On the table, there is a lamp.

There is a desk (**next to, between**) the table.
There is a chair (**in front of, behind**) the desk.
On the desk, there is a computer.

What is between the bed and the desk?
The (**table, chair**) is between the bed and the desk.

A Cat Below the Tree

Prepositions of Location

13 Key Words Read the words.

above

below

supermarket

post office

on the right

on the left

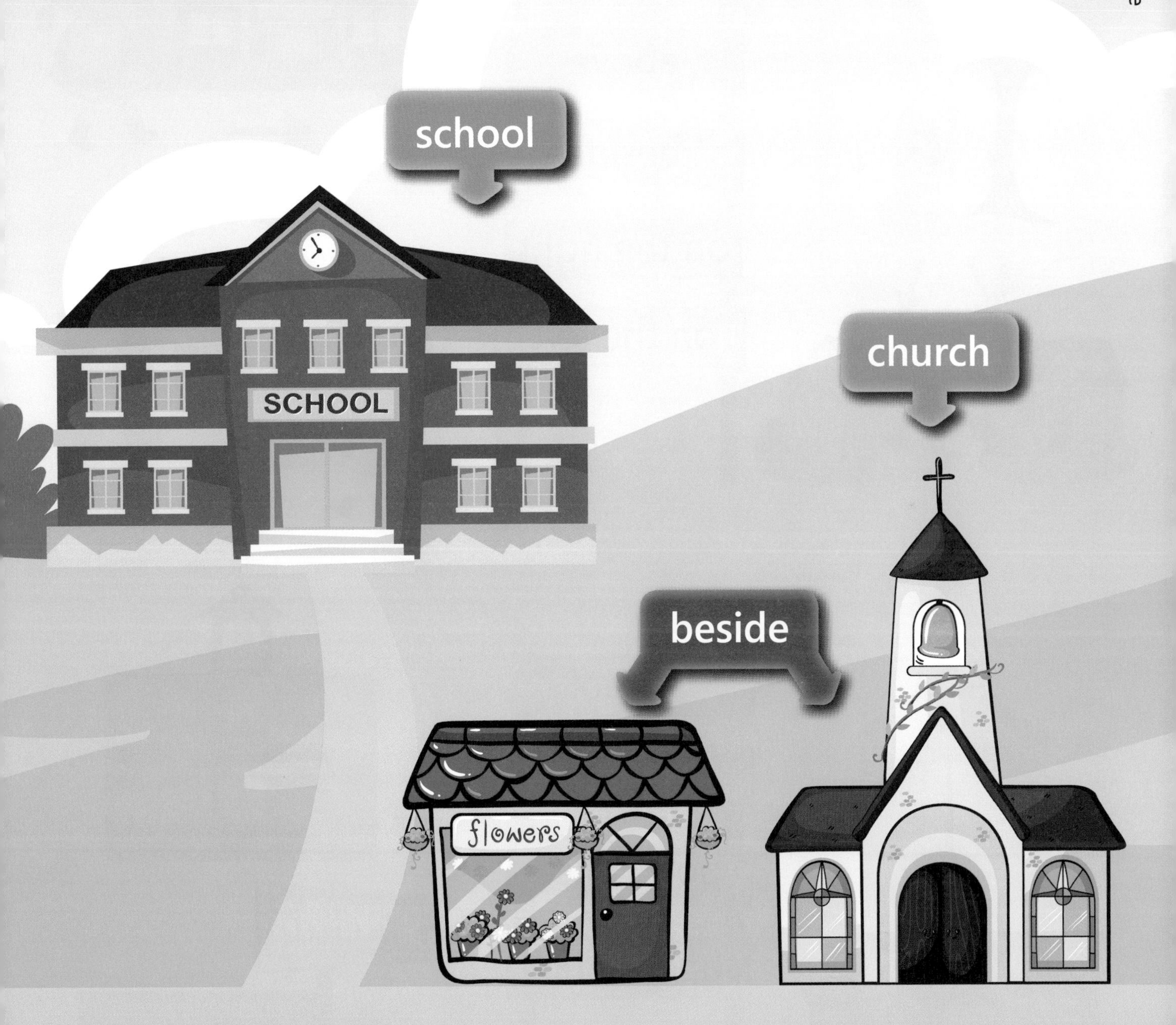
school
SCHOOL
church
beside
flowers

Match Up

Match the words with the pictures.

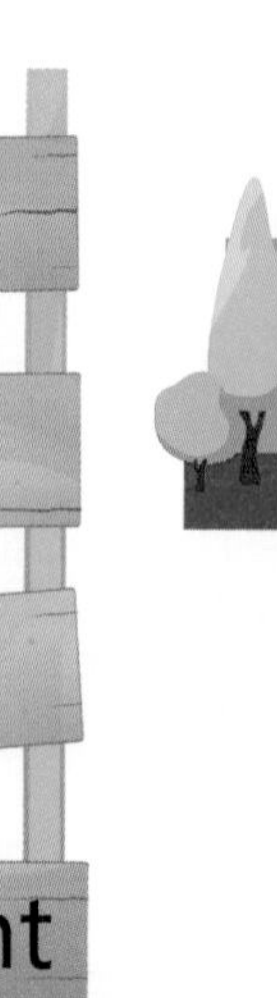

below

above

beside

on the right

on the left

school

church

post office

supermarket

Below or Above?

Circle the words **in blue**.

The bird is above the church.
The church is below the bird.

The school is next to the post office.
The school is by the post office.
The school is beside the post office.

On the Right or On the Left?

Circle the correct answer for each sentence.

The school is (**on the right**, **on the left**) of the post office.

The post office is (**on the right, on the left**) of the school.

The church is (**below, beside**) the school.

The church is (**between, beside**) the school and the post office.

Where Is Ann?

Circle the correct answer for each sentence.

Where is Ann?

She is (between, beside) the school and the supermarket.

Where is the school?

It is (**on the right, on the left**) of Ann.

Where is the supermarket?

It is (**on the right, on the left**) of Ann.

Where is the post office?

It is (**between, beside**) the supermarket.

I Can Read

Read the story.
Circle the words **in blue**.

This Is My Town.

I live in a small town.
There is a church beside my house.
The church is on the right of my house.
There is a post office on the right of the church.

There is a supermarket next to my house.
The supermarket is on the left of my house.
There is a school on the left of the supermarket.

There is a balloon above my house.
Can you find my house ?

UNIT 4

Inside and Outside

Prepositions of Location

bus stop

car

bus

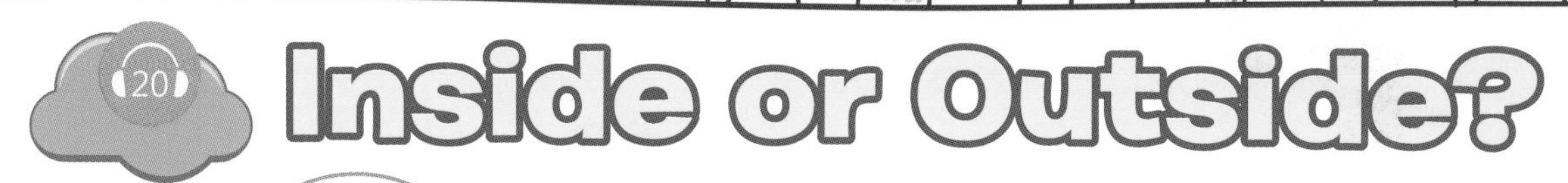

20 Inside or Outside?

Circle the correct answer for each sentence.

Tom is (**inside**, **outside**) the bus.

Ann is (**inside**, **outside**) the bus.

Jane is (**near**, **far from**) the bus stop.

John is (**near**, **far from**) the bus stop.

Where Is Tom?

Circle the correct answer for each sentence.

Where is Tom?

He is (**inside**, **outside**) the bus.

Where is Ann?

She is (**inside, outside**) the bus.

Where is John?

He is (**near, far from**) the bus stop.

Where is Jane?

She is (**near, far from**) the bus stop.

Is He?

Underline the words **is** and **isn't**.

Circle the words **Yes** and **No**.

Is he inside the car?

Yes, he is.

Is she outside the car?

Yes, she is.

Is he near the school?

No, he isn't.

Is she far from the school?

No, she isn't.

Where Is It?

Circle the correct answer for each sentence.

Where is the post office?

It is (**near**, **far from**) the bank.

Where is Jane?

She is (**inside, outside**) the post office.

SUPERMARKET

Where is Tom?

He is (**near, far from**) the post office.

Is Tom inside the supermarket?

No, he isn't.
He is (**inside, outside**) the supermarket.

I Can Read

Read the story. Find the friends and match.

Find the Friends.

This is Jane.
She is near the bus stop.

This is Ann.
She is far from the bus stop.

This is Sam.
He is outside the car.

This is Tom.
He is inside the car.

Review Test 1

A Choose and write.

in front of   between   behind   under   next to   on

B Circle the correct answer for each sentence.

1. The post office is (**on the right, on the left**) of the school.
2. The church is (**below, beside**) the school.
3. The bird is (**below, above**) the church.
4. The church is (**below, above**) the bird.

C Circle the correct answer for each sentence.

1. Where is Tom?
He is (inside, outside) the bus.

2. Where is the sofa?
It is (in, on) the living room.

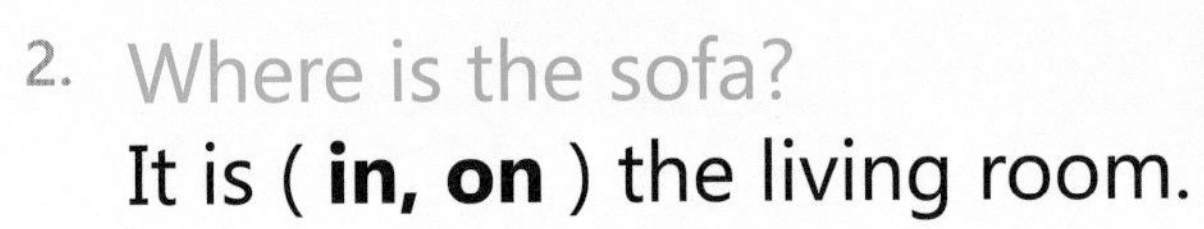

3. Where is the school?
It is (on the right, on the left) of Ann.

4. Where is the post office?
It is (between, beside) the supermarket.

D Match the sentences with the pictures.

1. Jane is near the bus stop. •

2. John is far from the bus stop. •

3. Ann is outside the car. •

4. Tom is inside the car. •

UNIT 5

Up and Down

Prepositions of Direction and Movement

25 **Key Words** Read the words.

stairs

elevator

pool

hill

26

Up or Down?

Circle the correct answer for each picture.

(go up, go down)

(go into, go out of)

(go into, go out of)

Go Up or Go Down?

Circle the correct word for each sentence.

He is going (up, **down**) the stairs.

She is going (**up, down**) the stairs.

The elevator is going (**up, down**).

The elevator is going (**up, down**).

The balloon is going (**up, down**).

Go Into or Go Out Of?

Circle the correct answer for each sentence.

She is going (into, out of) the school.

He is going (into, out of) the school.

She is going (into, out of) the pool.

He is going (into, out of) the pool.

What Is He Doing?

Circle the words with **-ing**.

What is she doing?

She is going up the stairs.

What is he doing?

He is going down the stairs.

What is she doing?

She is going into the pool.

What is he doing?

He is going out of the pool.

I Can Read

Read the story. Circle the words **in blue**.

What is Ben doing?

He is going up the hill.

What is Tom doing?

He is going down the hill.

What is Jane doing?

She is going into the water.

What is it doing?

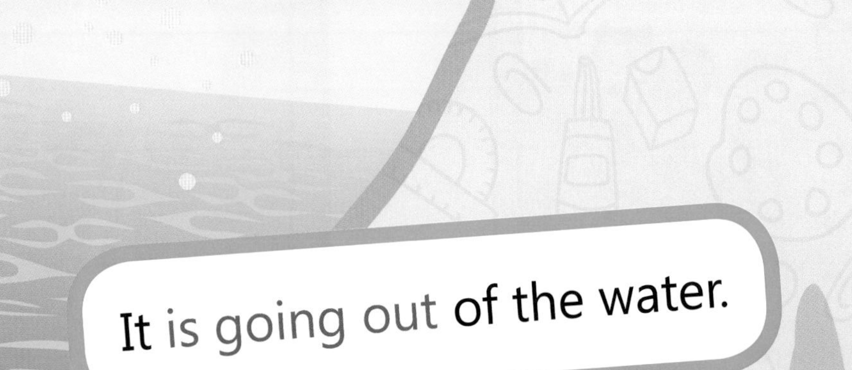

It is going out of the water.

Across and Over

Prepositions of Direction and Movement

Key Words Read the words.

across

around

over

through

street

corner
NO PARKING

track
4
5
6

tunnel
TUNNEL

Across or Around?

Circle the correct answer for each picture.

(go across, go around)

(go across, go around)

(go over, go through)

(go over, go through)

Go Across or Go Around?

Circle the correct word for each sentence.

She is going (**across**, **around**) the street.

He is going (**across**, **around**) the corner.

They are going (**across**, **around**) the street.

They are going (**across**, **around**) the track.

Go Over or Go Through?

Circle the correct word for each sentence.

He is going (**over**, **through**) the bar.

The bus is going (**over**, **through**) the gate.

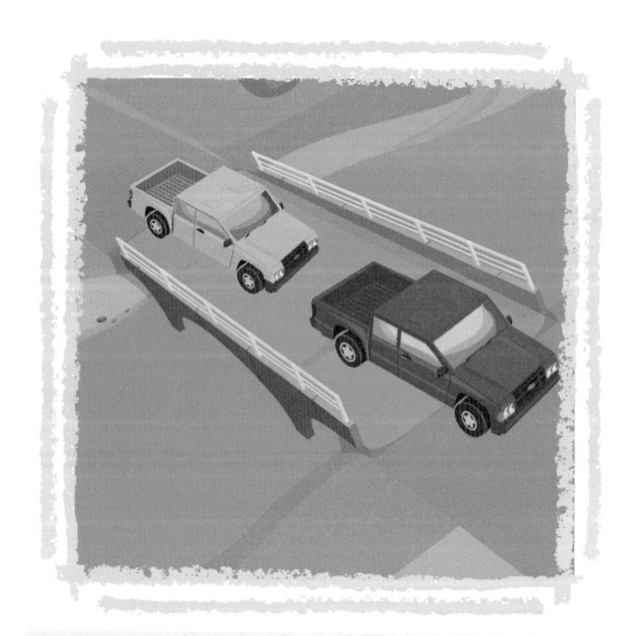

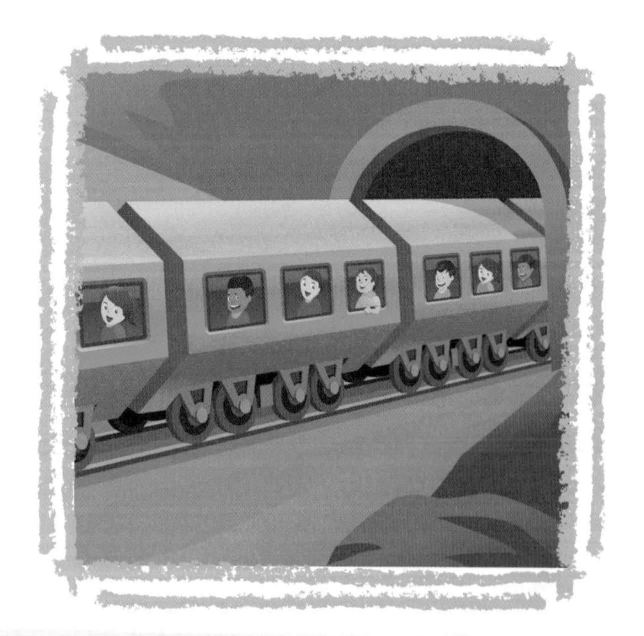

The cars are going (**over**, **through**) the bridge.

The train is going (**over**, **through**) the tunnel.

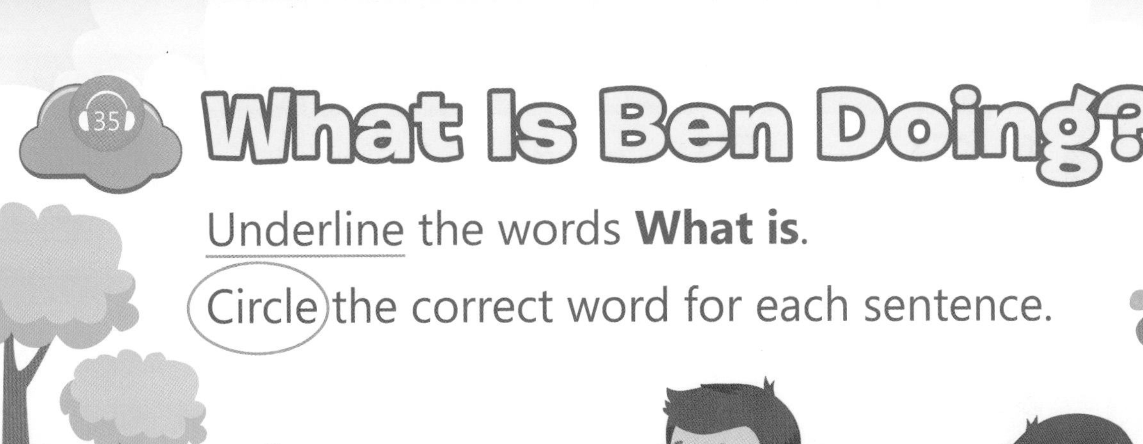

What Is Ben Doing?

Underline the words **What is**.

Circle the correct word for each sentence.

What is Ben doing?

He is going (**around**, **over**) the track.

What is Tom doing?

He is going (**around**, **over**) the bar.

What is Ann doing?

She is going (**through** , **around**) the finish line.

What is Jane doing?

Jane

She is going (**across**, **over**) the street.

I Can Read

Read the story. Circle the words **in blue**.

What are they doing?

They are going through the finish line.

What are they doing?

They are going around the corner.

What are they doing?

They are going across the snow field.

What are the cars doing?

They are going over the bridge.

In, On, At

Prepositions of Time

Key Words Read the words.

in

in the morning

in the afternoon

in the evening

on

on Monday

on Sunday

at

at 7 o'clock

at night

Match Up

Match the words with the pictures.

get up

have breakfast

have lunch

have dinner

go to school

go to church

go to bed

watch TV

In the Morning

Circle the correct word for each sentence.

I have breakfast in the (**morning**, **afternoon**).

I have lunch in the (**morning**, **afternoon**).

I have dinner in the (**morning**, **evening**).

I go to bed at (**night**, **morning**).

I Do

Circle the correct word for each sentence.

I go to school (**on**, **in**) Monday.

I go to church (**on**, **in**) Sunday.

I have lunch (**on**, **in**) the afternoon.

I get up (**at**, **in**) 7 o'clock.

I go to bed (**at**, **in**) night.

41 What Do You Usually Do?

Underline the words **What do you usually do**.

Match the sentences with the correct pictures.

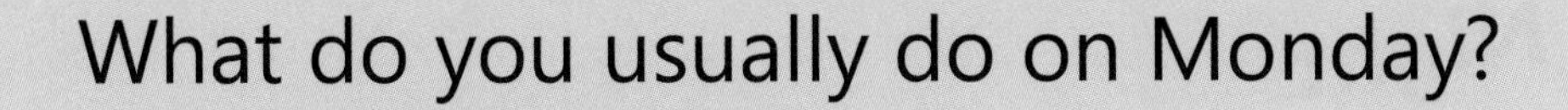

What do you usually do on Monday?

I go to school.

What do you usually do on Sunday?

I go to church.

What do you usually do in the morning?

I have breakfast.

What do you usually do at night?

I watch TV.

I Can Read

Read the story.

Match the sentences with the correct pictures.

Day and Night

It is day.
The sun shines during the day.
We go to school during the day.

It is night.
The moon shines at night.
We go to bed at night.

In and On

Prepositions of Time

Key Words Read the words.

in spring

in summer

Seasons

in fall

in winter

Special Days

on Christmas

on New Year's Day

on my birthday

Match Up

Match the words with the pictures.

go to the beach

go to the ski resort

go hiking

have a party

have a big meal

read a book

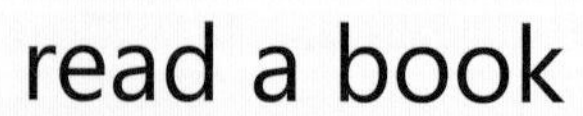

In Summer

Circle the correct word for each sentence.

I go hiking (**in**, **on**) spring.

I go to the beach (**in**, **on**) summer.

I go to the ski resort (**in**, **on**) winter.

I have a party (**in**, **on**) my birthday.

We have a big meal (**in**, **on**) New Year's Day.

We go to church (**in**, **on**) Christmas.

What Do You Usually Do?

Circle the correct word for each sentence.

Match the sentences with the correct pictures.

What do you usually do (in, on) spring?

I go hiking.

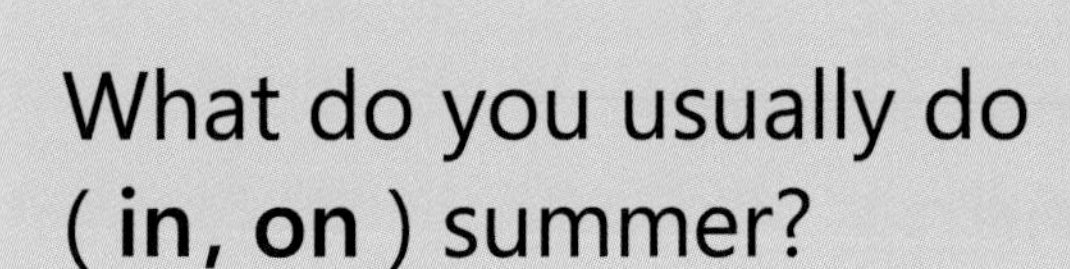

What do you usually do (in, on) summer?

I go to the beach.

What do you usually do (in, on) fall?

I read books.

What do you usually do (in, on) winter?

I go to the ski resort.

What Do People Usually Do?

Circle the correct word for each sentence.

Underline the word **They**.

What do people usually do (**in**, **on**) their birthdays?

They have a party.

What do people usually do (**in**, **on**) New Year's Day?

They have a big meal.

What do people usually do (**in**, **on**) summer?

They go to the beach.

What do people usually do (**in**, **on**) winter?

They go to the ski resort.

I Can Read

Read the story.
Check **Yes** or **No** for each sentence.

What Do People Usually Do?

People usually go to the ski resort in winter.

Yes No

People usually go to the beach in summer.

Yes No

People usually have a party on their birthdays.

Yes No

People usually have a big meal on New Year's Day.

Yes No

Review Test 2

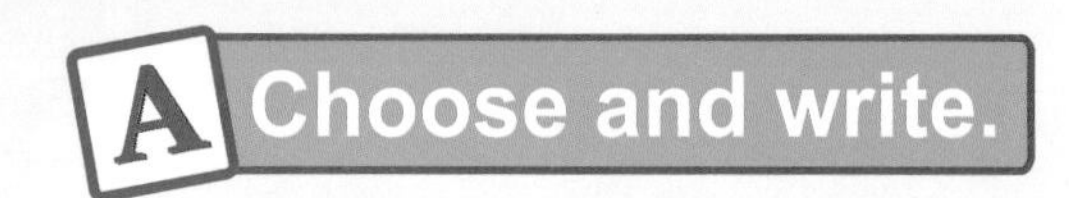

A Choose and write.

down up into out of have breakfast get up

B Circle the correct word for each sentence.

1. They are going (**through**, **around**) the finish line.
2. They are going (**through, around**) the corner.

3. He is going (**over, through**) the bar.

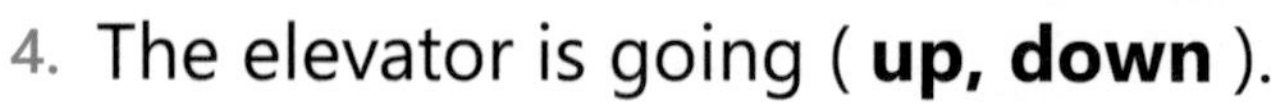

4. The elevator is going (**up, down**).

5. I usually go to the beach (**in, on**) summer.

6. I usually go to the ski resort in (**winter, spring**).

C Circle the correct word for each sentence.

1. 
What do people usually do (in, on) their birthdays?
They have a party.

2. 
What do you usually do (in, on) Monday?
I go to school.

3. 
What do you usually do (in, on) the morning?
I have breakfast.

4. 
What do you usually do (in, at) night?
I watch TV.

D Match the sentences with the pictures.

1. I go to church on Christmas.
2. We have a big meal on New Year's Day.
3. I go hiking in spring.
4. I read a book in the afternoon.
5. I get up at 7 o'clock.

Unit 1

A Cat In the Box
一隻貓在箱子裡

Prepositions of Location
表示地點的介系詞

1	**preposition**	介系詞
2	**location**	地點；位置
3	**in**	在……裡
4	**on**	在……上
5	**under**	在……的下面（正下方）
6	**by**	在……的旁邊
7	**box**	箱；盒
8	**basket**	籃；簍
9	**table**	桌子
10	**chair**	椅子
11	**There is**	有……（單數用）
12	**dog**	狗
13	**cat**	貓
14	**in the box**	在箱子裡
15	**on the box**	在箱子上面
16	**under the table**	在桌子下面
17	**by the table**	在桌子旁邊
18	**Where is . . . ?**	……在哪裡？（單數用）
19	**Where are . . . ?**	……在哪裡？(複數用)
20	**see**	看見；看到
21	**I see**	我看見……

Unit 2

A Cat Next To the Box
一隻貓在箱子的旁邊

Prepositions of Location
表示地點的介系詞

1	**in front of**	在……的前面
2	**behind**	在……的後面
3	**next to**	比鄰著……
4	**between**	在（兩個物品）……的中間
5	**bedroom**	臥室
6	**living room**	客廳
7	**sofa**	沙發；長椅

8 **behind the table** 在桌子的後面
9 **in front of the sofa** 在沙發的前面
10 **bed** 床
11 **next to the table** 在桌子旁邊
12 **lamp** 燈；油燈
13 **book** 書籍；書本
14 **between the books** 在書本中間
15 **This is** 這是……
16 **room** 房間；空間
17 **my room** 我的房間
18 **desk** 書桌；辦公桌
19 **computer** 電腦
20 **between A and B** 在 A 和 B 的中間
21 **between the bed and the desk** 在床和書桌的中間

Unit 3

A Cat Below the Tree
一隻貓在樹下

Prepositions of Location
表示地點的介系詞

1 **below** 在……下方（非正下方）
2 **above** 在……上方（非正上方）
3 **beside** 在……旁邊
4 **on the right** 在右邊
5 **on the left** 在左邊
6 **school** 學校
7 **church** 教堂
8 **post office** 郵局
9 **supermarket** 超級市場
10 **bird** 鳥
11 **above the church** 在教堂的上方
12 **below the bird** 在鳥的下方
13 **beside the post office** 在郵局的旁邊
14 **on the right of** 在……的右邊
15 **on the right of the post office** 在郵局的右邊
16 **on the left of** 在……的左邊
17 **on the left of the school** 在學校的左邊
18 **town** 鎮；市鎮
19 **my town** 我的城鎮
20 **live in** 住在……
21 **small** 小的
22 **house** 房子；住宅
23 **balloon** 氣球；氫氣球
24 **Can you . . . ?** 你可以……嗎？
25 **find** 找到；發現

Unit 4

Inside and Outside
在裡面，在外面

Prepositions of Location
表示地點的介系詞

1 **inside** 在……裡面

2 **outside** 在……外面

3 **near** 在……附近

4 **far from** 離……很遠

5 **bus stop** 公車站

6 **car** 汽車

7 **bus** 公車；巴士

8 **inside the bus** 在公車裡

9 **outside the bus** 在公車外面

10 **near the bus stop** 在公車站附近

11 **far from the bus stop** 離公車站很遠

12 **Is he . . . ?** 他是……嗎？

13 **Is he inside the car?** 他在公車裡嗎？

14 **Yes, he is.** 對，他在公車裡。

15 **No, he isn't.** 不，他不在公車裡。

16 **bank** 銀行

17 **friend** 朋友

18 **This is** 這是……

Unit 5

Up and Down
往上，往下

Prepositions of Direction and Movement

表示移動方向的介系詞

1 **direction** 方向；方位

2 **movement** 動作

3 **up** 往上

4 **down** 往下

5 **into** 進入……（某處）

6 **out of** 離開……（某處）

7 **stairs** 樓梯

8 **elevator** 電梯；升降機

9 **pool** 游泳池

10 **hill** 小山；丘陵

11 **go** 去

12 **go up** 上升

13 **go down** 下降

14 **go into** 進入……

15 **go out of** 離開……；出去……

16 **is going** 正在往……

17 **is going up** 正在往上

18 **is going up the stairs** 正走上樓梯

19 **is going down** 正在往下

20 **is going down the stairs** 正走下樓梯

21 **into the school** 進入學校

22 **is going into the school** 正進入學校

23 **out of the school** 離開學校

24 **is going out of the school** 正離開學校

25 **What is . . . doing?** ……正在做什麼？

26 **What is he doing?** 他正在做什麼？

27 **What is she doing?** 她正在做什麼？

28 **is going up the hill**
正在上山坡

29 **is going down the hill**
正在下山坡

30 **is going into the water**
正進入水裡

31 **is going out of the water**
正離開水裡

Unit 6

Across and Over
橫越，越過（一個高起的物品）

Prepositions of Direction and Movement
表示移動方向的介系詞

1 **across** 橫越
2 **around** 環繞
3 **over** 越過（一個高起的物品）
4 **through** 穿越；通過
5 **street** 街道
6 **corner** 角；街角
7 **track** 跑道；小徑；小道
8 **tunnel** 隧道
9 **go across** 走過……
10 **go around** 繞過……
11 **go over** 越過……
12 **go through** 穿過……
13 **across the street** 橫越街道
14 **around the corner** 繞過轉角
15 **around the track** 繞過跑道
16 **bar** 欄杆；衡桿
17 **over the bar** 越過欄杆
18 **gate** 大門；出入口
19 **through the gate** 穿過大門
20 **bridge** 橋；橋樑
21 **over the bridge** 越過橋樑
22 **train** 火車；列車
23 **through the tunnel** 穿過隧道
24 **finish line** 終點線
25 **through the finish line** 穿越終點線
26 **snow field** 雪原
27 **across the snow field** 橫越雪原

Unit 7

In, On, At
在，在，在

Prepositions of Time
表示時間的介系詞

1 **time** 時間
2 **in** 在……(一天中的某一時段)
3 **morning** 早晨；上午
4 **afternoon** 下午；午後
5 **evening** 傍晚；晚上
6 **in the morning** 在早上
7 **in the afternoon** 在下午

8 **in the evening** 在晚上
9 **on** 在⋯⋯（星期；日期）
10 **Monday** 星期一
11 **Sunday** 星期日
12 **on Monday** 在星期一
13 **on Sunday** 在星期日
14 **at**
在⋯⋯（一天中的一個確切時間）
15 **7 o'clock** 七點鐘
16 **night** 晚上
17 **at 7 o'clock** 在七點鐘
18 **at night** 在晚上
19 **get up** 起床
20 **have** 吃；喝
21 **breakfast** 早餐
22 **lunch** 午餐
23 **dinner** 晚餐
24 **have breakfast** 吃早餐
25 **have lunch** 吃午餐
26 **have dinner** 吃晚餐
27 **go to** 前往⋯⋯
28 **go to school** 前往學校
29 **go to church** 前往教堂
30 **go to bed** 上床睡覺
31 **watch TV** 看電視
32 **do** 做
33 **I do** 我做⋯⋯
34 **usually** 通常
35 **What do you usually do?**
你通常做什麼？
36 **day** 白天；日
37 **night** 晚上；夜
38 **It is day.** 現在是白天。
39 **the sun** 太陽
40 **shine** 照耀；發光
41 **during** 在⋯⋯期間
42 **during the day** 在白天期間
43 **It is night.** 現在是晚上。
44 **the moon** 月亮

Unit 8

In and On
在，在

Prepositions of Time
表示時間的介系詞

1 **season** 季節
2 **in** 在⋯⋯（季節）
3 **spring** 春天
4 **summer** 夏天
5 **fall** 秋天
6 **winter** 冬天
7 **in spring** 在春天
8 **in summer** 在夏天
9 **in fall** 在秋天
10 **in winter** 在冬天

11	**special**	特別的；特殊的
12	**special day**	特別日
13	**on**	在……（特別日）
14	**Christmas**	聖誕節
15	**New Year's Day**	元旦
16	**birthday**	生日
17	**on Christmas**	在聖誕節
18	**on New Year's Day**	在元旦
19	**on my birthday**	在我的生日
20	**beach**	海灘
21	**go to the beach**	前往海灘
22	**ski resort**	滑雪場
23	**go to the ski resort**	前往滑雪場
24	**go hiking**	徒步旅行
25	**party**	派對；舞會
26	**have a party**	舉辦派對
27	**meal**	一餐
28	**a big meal**	一頓大餐
29	**have a big meal**	吃一頓大餐
30	**read a book**	讀一本書
31	**people**	人們

32 **What do people usually do?**
人們通常做什麼？

國家圖書館出版品預行編目資料

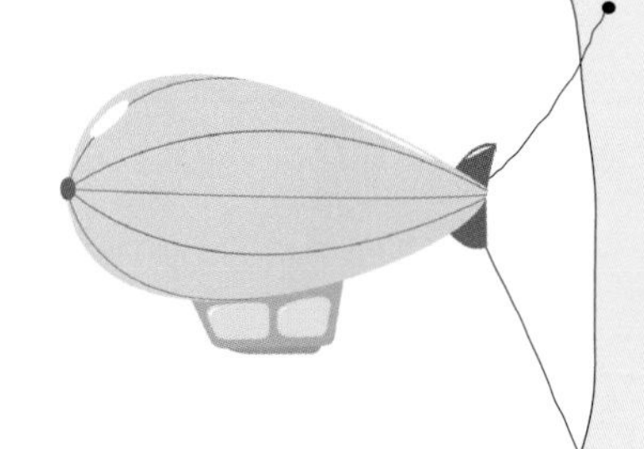

Fun 學美國各學科 Preschool 閱讀課本．4，介系詞篇 / Michael A. Putlack, e-Creative Contents 著；歐寶妮譯．-- 二版．--［臺北市］：寂天文化，2018.11
面； 公分

ISBN 978-986-318-751-6（平裝附光碟片）

1. 英語 2. 介詞
805.1664 107018727

FUN學美國各學科

Preschool 閱讀課本 4 介系詞篇 二版

作　　者 Michael A. Putlack & e-Creative Contents
譯　　者 歐寶妮
編　　輯 呂敏如／歐寶妮
主　　編 丁宥暄
內文排版 洪伊珊
封面設計 林書玉
製程管理 洪巧玲
出 版 者 寂天文化事業股份有限公司
電　　話 02-2365-9739
傳　　真 02-2365-9835
網　　址 www.icosmos.com.tw
讀者服務 onlineservice@icosmos.com.tw
出版日期 2018 年 11 月 二版一刷 080201

郵撥帳號 1998620-0 **寂天文化事業股份有限公司**
劃撥金額 600（含）元以上者，郵資免費。
訂購金額 600 元以下者，加收 65 元運費。
〔若有破損，請寄回更換，謝謝〕